MYSTERIUM
黑 THE BLACK DRAGON 龍

Coming soon . . .

The Mysterium

Danny's story continues in . . .

The Palace of Memory
(January 2014)

The Wheel of Life and Death
(July 2014)

JULIAN SEDGWICK

the MYSTERIUM

黑 THE BLACK DRAGON 龍

Hodder
Children's
Books

A division of Hachette Children's Books

A Catalogue record for this book is available from the British Library

ISBN 978 1 444 91370 5

Typeset in Garamond Book by Avon DataSet Ltd,
Bidford-on-Avon, Warwickshire

Printed and bound by CPI Group (UK) Ltd, Croydon, CR0 4YY

The paper and board used in this paperback by Hodder Children's Books
are natural recyclable products made from wood grown in
sustainable forests. The manufacturing processes conform to the
environmental regulations of the country of origin.

Hodder Children's Books
a division of Hachette Children's Books
338 Euston Road, London NW1 3BH
An Hachette UK company
www.hachette.co.uk

For Joe and Will. Of course.

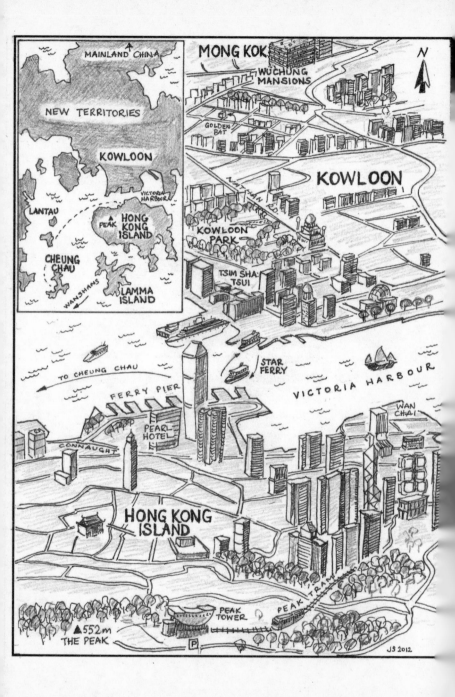

ACT ONE

Life is being on the wire.
Everything else is just waiting.

Karl Wallenda

1 HOW TO SURVIVE

Danny Woo opens his eyes.

The left one is electric green, the right a deep, chestnut brown. Intense and brooding, they gaze out into the October morning.

'Oi, Woo! You going to show us your stupid card trick or what?'

Danny groans inwardly as Jamie G leans over him. 'Now?'

'Got time, Freaky. Unless you're scared of missing the bell.'

Danny shakes his head and takes the magician's deck from his trouser pocket. Heartbeat thickening, he shuffles the cards and cuts. It must work, he thinks. I must get it right – or face more rubbish from Jamie and his mates. He remembers this very same pack sliding through Dad's practised fingers. Hard to believe. Concentrate, Danny.

He draws a breath, steadies his hands as the others

gather to watch. The raucous noise of the changing rooms ebbs away to an expectant hush.

'OK. Pick a card,' he says, fanning the deck, holding them out face down, and – yes – the timing of the 'force' is perfect. As if drawn by a magnet, Jamie plucks out the King of Spades as planned. Good.

'Look at it,' Danny says. 'All of you take a look.'

That gives him the vital half-second he needs to get the rubber band in place, tucked behind the deck.

'Put it back. Wherever you want.' Except that's not true. It must be in just the right place.

Jamie shoves the card back, trying to throw him, but Danny gets his little finger in place – a perfectly disguised 'pinky break' – and snicks the elastic band around the corner of the King. He tightens the deck. Maybe it hasn't quite caught? No going back now.

'Think about your card. Say it over and over in your head.' He holds the pack at arm's length, eyes burning into their backs, then snaps his little finger towards him, hidden from the others. But the band slips, and instead of jumping, the King does no more than jut up a fraction, before stopping dead. Damn it.

Danny pulls it from the deck, putting on a brave face as he shows his audience. 'King of Spades, right?'

'Uh huh.' Jamie curls his lip, trying not to look impressed. 'You got it. Now show it me again, Freaky.'

'No,' Danny says, thinking of what Dad would say. Never *repeat*. Never *explain* . . .

'Then I'll show you my own trick, Woo,' Jamie says. He snatches the deck and hurls it into the air. 'Fifty-flipping-two-card pick-up! Catch!'

The others laugh as Danny scrabbles to retrieve the cards from the changing room floor. He can smell disinfectant on the tiles, sterile and cold. He's been boarding at Ballstone for over a year, but still the place gives him the creeps. How different from the Mysterium and its heady aroma of wet grass, dry ice, burning paraffin, thunderclap smoke, greasepaint – the vital, living scent of the big top when you unrolled it at a new venue. But that's all gone. And he's got to get used to that.

He picks the cards up one by one, counting them to make sure they're all there.

And now he's late for the next lesson.

Danny runs after the others, needing to make up time or face another mind-numbing detention. His slim form darts across the main courtyard, overtaking Jamie and the rest. He glances at his watch – only a fraction past ten thirty. Should be OK.

The rooks are calling darkly overhead, flapping away at their nests in the elm trees. Danny's fingers reach for the door—

—and then the explosion rocks the building to its foundations.

It flashes on Danny's face, whites out his vision.

The blast wave follows a split second later, thumping down the corridor, blowing out the doors, sending him sprawling across the tarmac. He knows how to fall and roll, but there's no time to prepare. His face strikes the tarmac hard and he flops over twice, before lying there stunned, listening as the explosion dies away in a long, drawn-out growl.

Stars dance in his head. The air is full of smoke and the stench of smouldering electrics – and it feels like all the breath has been sucked from his lungs.

In his mouth there's the iron tang of blood, and when he reaches up to check, his fingertips come away red. Sitting up, his mind blank for a moment, he tries to work out what has happened. It takes a minute or so to remember where he is. Who he is! He sees Jamie and the others staggering around looking equally dazed.

Paper from the noticeboards floats down around

them like oversized, charred snowflakes. One sheet, half crisped, brushes his cheek – and instinctively he reaches up to catch it. Instead of carrying the school's logo and usual heading, it's almost blank. In the middle of what's left is a small diagram of sorts: a neat grid of black dots, seven rows by seven columns. One of them – second row down on the left-hand side – is circled in red pen.

The dots swim in his vision, eyes watering.

Under the diagram someone has written '1030': the numbers are heavily done, pressed down into the paper.

Nothing else.

He looks at it for a moment, but, like so much in his life right now, it makes no sense at all. Absent-mindedly, he folds the paper and shoves it in his back pocket.

Through the smoke he can see the rooks wheeling overhead, shaken from the trees by the explosion. They cackle and caw, ragged black crosses against the sky.

2 HOW TO BE FULLY ALIVE

By a fluke the main corridor was empty when the explosion hit, and so there are no major casualties – just nasty cuts and bruises from flying debris, and a few students suffering from shock. They sit around the courtyard, dazed, wrapped in reflective blankets, while the emergency services put up yellow tape and walkie-talkies crackle the air with static.

Danny is assessed by a paramedic. She asks if he banged his head, and gets him to follow her finger with his eyes, before shining a torch deep into them.

'Pupils dilating fine. Nice colours!' she adds with a smile. 'You get them from Mum and Dad? One from each?'

Danny does his best to smile back, but as the medic dresses the cut, she notices that his eyes don't join in. The rest of the face is almost frozen.

'You OK now? Sure?'

'Yes. Thanks.'

'Well, take it easy, young man. Watch out for shock.'

'What does it feel like?'

'Like you're locked up tight. Can't get moving.'

He nods. But isn't that what he's been feeling each and every day this last year and a half?

Classes are suspended until further notice and Danny retreats to the sanctuary of the room that – thankfully – he has to himself. He flops on the bed and stares at the cracks in the ceiling. A few minutes earlier and—

No, it doesn't bear thinking about. He shakes his head to clear the thought.

But there's more to cope with than that. The acrid smell of the explosion, the cold weather, the arrival of the emergency services are all conspiring to remind him of *that* terrible day twenty long months ago: snow falling steadily from the Berlin sky, shock tearing his insides as the policeman pulled him away from the charred, broken remains of their circus trailer. The ambulance unloading stretchers for Mum and Dad. Or what was left of them.

He shudders. Tries to push the thoughts back down and lock them away again. Like normal.

But this time it's different.

The memories refuse to lie down again. And vaguely he's aware that the blast has shaken something loose. Agitation rises up in waves – as if waking him from a long but fitful night's sleep. The feeling keeps growing; an impulse to get moving, to be *doing* something. Unable to rest, he starts to pace the room like Dad used to do when struggling to perfect an escape, eager to eat his dinner and get back to the practice ring.

'Woo!' Jamie breezes in without knocking, throwing himself down in an armchair. The knowing smirk temporarily knocked from the corners of his mouth.

'Did you hear? It was a gas leak, and now there's no heating. Old Kircher's shutting early for half term. Result or what?!'

'What are you doing in my room? What do you want?'

Jamie ignores the question. 'If I hadn't chucked your stupid cards . . .' He lets the thought hang for a moment. 'I saved your life, Woo! You could thank me.'

'Yep. Thanks.'

'Were you scared?'

'Not really.' And strangely enough that's the truth, Danny thinks.

'I nearly crapped myself!'

The smirk's coming back as Jamie's eyes rove the room. They latch onto a framed photo on Danny's desk: it shows a powerfully built dwarf standing beside an oversized cannon. He's dressed in an astronaut outfit, his head shaved close and muscles bulging through his silver spacesuit. Tucked under his arm is a helmet marked with a big red Z.

Danny follows Jamie's gaze, and sees his eleven-year-old self standing in the picture beside the dwarf – smiling, looking relaxed. Only a year and a half ago, but it seems like a hundred. Even the little quiff in his short dark hair looks perkier there.

'And who's this little freak you're with?'

'Major Zamora. Our strongman,' Danny says, biting back anger. 'That's his old human cannonball act – Captain Solaris.'

'Bet they fired him,' Jamie says, laughing at his own joke.

As if no one's ever told that one before! How to explain to an idiot like Jamie Gunn? How to say just how important Zamora has been: lifelong friend, confidant, godfather . . . all rolled into one. Danny has missed Zamora almost as much as Mum and Dad. And it's been ages. The one chance he had to see the dwarf again had been on a tour of Zamora's latest outfit – Circo Micro – but being up close to the circus world again had felt too raw.

'He's what? A midget?' Jamie says.

'A dwarf. Midget's rude.'

'So your circus was all freak shows, animal cruelty?'

'No! Never heard of Archaos? Cirque du Soleil?'

'Nah.'

'That's "new circus". Just like us. Scary, arty. Edgy stuff. No animals—'

'Circus is just for kids,' Jamie says with a snort. 'And what did your folks do, then?'

'Amazing things . . .'

Danny's still lost in the photo. You can just see part of his old trailer home in the background, and the memories come bubbling up – both good and bad. How to describe the wild beauty of the Mysterium and its band of misfits, loners, dreamers? Jamie G won't understand, so no point trying to explain. You had to see it to believe it.

'Gotta go, Freaky,' Gunn says, getting up to leave. 'What're you going to do with the extra holiday then?'

'Just going to be at Aunt Laura's, I guess.'

'Well, have fun, woncha?'

Jamie being nice? Just another bit of weirdness to add to the day.

* * *

Phone calls are made to announce the closure, and Danny goes to wait for Aunt Laura in the common room. For some reason he can't fathom, the windows there are barred. Keeping people out – or in? Through them he can see the mud-locked games pitches, and, beyond them, the high wall that circles the school cutting into the mist.

Still he can't settle, and, impatiently, he goes to stand on the front steps. Maybe it's just the adrenalin rush from the explosion punching through his system. Maybe. But there's something deeper there now, pushing him towards action, movement. Come on, Laura. Get a move on.

And then suddenly she's powering up the driveway, her old Citroën chewing up the gravel. He watches as Laura brakes hard, sliding the car between an ambulance and a smart Jag, missing both by a whisker.

She jumps out, takes in the column of smoke drifting heavenwards from the back of the school, and, mouth dropping open in concern, comes striding across the fire hoses. Without thought for any embarrassment she might cause, she throws her arms hard around him. She takes her role as guardian seriously, and puts every ounce of strength into the hug.

'Danny! My God. Are you OK?'

'I'm fine,' he says, wriggling free.

'So what's this bandage?'

She breaks off, holding his shoulders, appraising him at arm's length. For an investigative journalist – a fearless one at that, who takes everything in her stride – she suddenly seems knocked off balance. Even the short stint in prison didn't do that to her.

'God! A minute earlier and—'

'I'm OK,' he says. 'I just want to get going.'

'Well, I've got a thing or two to say to your blasted head first. What's his name again?'

'Mr Kircher.'

'Kircher. Right! You go and pack your stuff.'

'Aunt Laura—' he calls after her, but it's no use. She's marching through the front doors to tackle the head.

'Kircher, a word or two, if you please. No, I haven't got time to wait! You're lucky we don't pursue a negligence claim. How'd you like that in the papers to make you choke on your bloody cornflakes!'

No contest.

Danny watches her go as Kircher takes a defensive step backwards. This is more like the usual Aunt Laura

– a box of fireworks, ready to take on anyone, anything.

He heads to pack, mulling things over as he goes. Maybe I should get out the posters of Mum and Dad from under the bed when I come back, he thinks. Put them up. Maybe it would help. But then people like Jamie would just mock them. And maybe it's still too painful.

They can stay where they are, rolled up – protected and safe – in their cardboard tubes: Mum strolling on the wire, under the very highest point of the Mysterium's midnight-blue 'hemisphere', tossing firecrackers to the ground far below, the poster emblazoned with the words LILY WOO in the *WONDER CHAMBER*.

And the beautiful painted one of Dad at the end of his burning rope, bound in the straitjacket, flames chewing his ankles as he turns to smile at the audience, oblivious of the danger. THE GREAT HARRY WHITE, it says. HE CAN ESCAPE FROM ANYTHING!

Except it wasn't true, was it?

Danny sets about putting cards, magic books, home clothes into his old circus trunk. It's the same dark blue as their old big top, and proudly carries the single word MYSTERIUM.

Underneath that is the logo: a pure-white skull

gazing out of the darkness, surrounded by pale-blue and red butterflies. Dad had said it was a kind of vanitas – an image that contained at once both death and fragile life, to remind you how everything changes, is transient. And one day gone forever.

'*A whisker away from nothingness, Danny.*'

'*So why do we have it on our logo?*'

'*Because that's what it's all about. Being fully alive! By not forgetting that we're lucky to be here at all!*'

Danny runs his finger over the golden letters now. Everything is changing. All the time. Maybe it would have been better to have parents who commuted to work and nagged you about homework and did normal things and expected you to do the same.

He sighs. Maybe.

From the bottom drawer of his desk, he takes Dad's thick notebook and lays it on the clothes. It's just smaller than A4 in size, and stuffed with working notes, drawings, newspaper clippings, photos, diagrams and lists. On the cover, in strong capitals:

THE MYSTERIUM
ESCAPE BOOK
SECRET

Danny shuts the lid and snaps the padlock shut. The sides of the trunk are covered in stickers, listing the places he's seen: Rome, Athens, Budapest, Bordeaux, Lisbon, Paris, Buenos Aires, Santiago, Munich and on and on – one tour after another. There, tucked amongst them, the last one he stuck to the side: Berlin.

No more stickers after that.

'Ready then, Danny boy?' Laura says brightly, popping her head in the door. 'Let's move it! And I've got a surprise for you.'

3 HOW TO GET AN UPGRADE FOR FREE

But on the drive back to Cambridge, Laura falls silent. Danny knows she's thinking something through by the way she tilts her head slightly one way, then another – clearly weighing up options. She accelerates to overtake a string of lorries and glances back at him.

'So, what's this surprise?' he asks.

'Well. I was thinking. How about a change of scene? Take your mind off things? I'm up to here with research for my Hong Kong story.' She forces a smile, and sweeps the blonde hair from her eyes. 'Thought I might fly out earlier than I meant to and . . . And, well, perhaps take you with me? God knows if school will re-open on time. I doubt it very much.'

'Hong Kong?!'

'Why not? You've always wanted to go, haven't you? See where Lily came from – God rest her soul. It might help.'

'I don't know.'

On the one hand he just wants to stay put. Enjoy that quiet, cosy half term as usual, surrounded by the salvaged stuff from the Mysterium. Tuck up in his attic room with the Houdini biography and watch YouTube clips of David Blaine and people like that. Afternoons poring over the *Escape Book* maybe, trying to crack the many coded entries.

On the other hand – Hong Kong, Mum's birthplace? Actually doing something rather than holing up, nursing his wounds.

'Thought you'd jump at it,' Laura says.

The thought of travel *does* chime with that urge for action and movement . . .

'And I'd appreciate the company, Danny boy! Some of these gangs I'm investigating are scary as hell.'

'So would I be helping?'

'God no. You'll be sightseeing. Having a good time.'

'On my own?'

'You'll need a companion,' Laura says, playing her trump card. 'A minder, if you like. Someone trustworthy. Someone whose shoulders we can rely on?' A smile flickers on her lips. 'Someone like . . . Major Zamora, for example?'

He has guessed as much before she says it. After all, a dwarf who can lift a motorbike over his head? Now, *those* are reliable shoulders. Pinned to Danny's bedroom wall are the postcards Zamora has sent as he drifts from one contract to another. Pictures of Paris, the Acropolis in Athens, the Trevi Fountain in Rome.

And now? Somewhere new and unrelated to the Mysterium? Danny feels his face lifting. And to see Hong Kong at last . . .

Laura glances at him again. 'I'll take that smile as a "yes" then.'

She pushes hard on the accelerator and the Citroën leaps into the fading light.

'Yes.'

From around his neck, hung on a bootlace, Danny takes his talisman: Dad's lockpick set – one of the few items that survived the fire. Five slender picks and a detachable tension tool folded into a stainless-steel handle. Goodness only knows how many locks Dad picked with the thing. He looks at it for a moment as it turns slowly on the bootlace, rolling the names of the tools in his head: snake rake, half diamond, hook pick, double round. It's like a prayer saying those words. A prayer of escape. And maybe it's being answered.

It's dark by the time they reach home. Laura drives past a parking place right outside the house.

'You missed a space.'

'Dammit,' she sighs, weaving into another one, some twenty houses further down the street. 'Wasn't concentrating.'

But before she unlocks the front door, she throws a quick look over her shoulder. There's something hyperalert in her eyes. Checking to see if someone or something's there? Even though Danny is glad to be back – even though he feels the reassurance of his own room beckoning – he's alert enough to catch that glance.

'Come on, Danny boy!' Laura calls, disabling the alarm.

He turns and scans the street. Nothing to see. Just a frost blinding the car windscreens. Imagination getting the better of me maybe, he thinks, and turns to head up to his room.

'Chuck your school clothes in the basket,' Laura says. 'We'll wash them when we get back.'

Deep in his back pocket the charred piece of paper with the diagram lies forgotten. The question he meant to ask forgotten with it.

21

Two days later they are standing in a check-in queue at
Heathrow Terminal 5.

Laura has arranged everything smoothly, effortlessly,
by her standards. Normally she would flail around and
misplace something and make ten phone calls – and
then find the thing she was looking for in the first
place. To Danny it's almost as if the change of flight
and his inclusion has been anticipated. Her behaviour
is a bit out of character, and although – for the first
time in ages – excitement is building inside him, he
keeps a watchful eye on her.

Laura is studying the e-ticket, pulling a face. 'Jeez, I
wish the newspaper could have stumped up for premium
economy. I need to work a bit. And get some sleep.'

She looks at Danny's small bag on the floor. 'Sure
you've got enough?'

'Never had much on tour. Dad always said too
many things—'

'—stop you living properly. Yeah, I heard it!
Too often!'

Danny has packed light – cards, iPod, a few clothes.
The *Escape Book* nearly came too, but much safer to
leave that at home. There'll be time to trawl its coded
secrets later.

Laura looks ruefully at her own bags bursting with notebooks, camera equipment, files. As she shuffles towards the desk, kicking one holdall in front of her, she turns her head. That same quick glance, senses alert, just like the other night. Something's up, but what? He looks round to follow her gaze, but again there is nothing unusual to see on the wide, bright concourse.

'Are you OK, Aunt Laura?'

'*Perfecto*. Hey, our turn!'

The BA attendant at the counter smiles her made-up smile at Danny, comparing his passport photo with his face.

'Danny Woo? Going home then?'

How to answer that? The Mysterium trailer *was* home, even if it was a home that moved every week. But now that's gone. And 'home' certainly isn't Ballstone. Or Laura's house – not quite. I'm not that same boy any more, not the circus boy who watched Mum and Dad and the rest of them. And I'm not a Ballstone student either. Not really.

Feels like he is always defending himself at school from being typecast as some weirdo outsider or a grief-stricken orphan straight out of some Victorian novel.

If I don't fit anywhere, then who am I?

23

'You must know where home is, young man!'

There's something patronizing in her manner and it spurs him on to try something. Do Laura a favour. OK. Animate your face like Dad used to do. Get the woman on side.

'Sort of going home,' he says. 'It's my mum's name. It's a tradition to take your mother's surname where she came from.'

'Oh, really? Where's that?'

'Chinese circus.'

'Fancy that!'

'But our circus was in Europe. The Mysterium,' he says, keeping firm eye contact, making sure she can see their glowing colours.

'Goodness me.'

'We went everywhere. Germany, Italy, America . . .'

Bit by bit, he starts to mirror the movements she's making with her eyes, eyebrows. When her hand reaches up to scratch her forehead, he mimics her, and when she reaches down to the keyboard, he does the same.

Laura is rummaging away in her leather shoulder bag. 'Bloody hell, where did I put my passport?'

The BA lady hesitates, glancing uncertainly back at Danny. Now's the moment. He opens his eyes wide and looks deep into her pupils. Then waves his hand across them. 'We upgraded yesterday. Booking ref IS4JS,' he says.

The woman checks her screen and, as she does so, he raps hard on the counter with his knuckles. 'To *business* class,' he says, voice ringing with conviction.

Laura opens her mouth, but he kicks her foot under the counter – and she quietly hands over her own passport. The check-in lady blinks a couple of times, taps the keyboard – then blinks again.

'. . . So you have. I think. Business class. How nice. Here are your boarding passes.'

They head for security leaving the woman looking at her screen, puzzled. Danny feels a glow taking hold of him, a spring in his step, like he's grown a few centimetres. I did it, he thinks. Just like it's supposed to go.

'Bad boy,' Laura says, smiling. 'One of your dad's tricks, I suppose?'

'It's a "mirror force". You just copy their breathing, movements, that kind of thing, until they feel really relaxed.' He shrugs. 'Then hit them with the suggestion. Never works on teachers though.'

'What about your friends?'

Danny is putting the lockpick set in the plastic tray.

He shrugs again. Friends? There are people he can chat to at school. But no one you could really call a 'friend'. Not like the ones he had in the Mysterium. Friendship in the circus was vital, a serious business, Mum always said. You had to trust – and be trusted – to walk a wire or be chainsawed in half by your husband.

Laura watches him as he slips through the arch of the metal detector, contained, wrapped in his thoughts. Listed on the back of his Mysterium tour T-shirt are the dates for that last fateful show – *WONDER CHAMBER*. A roll call of European cities in block capitals that tick away the days and venues to BERLIN and – after that – all the places that were destined never to be played. After the tragedy, the company parted and ceased to exist in anything other than memory.

She frowns hard, holding back her own emotion for a moment, and then follows him through the gateway of the scanner. This is the right thing to do, she thinks, trying, but not quite succeeding, to convince herself.

4 HOW TO TRAVEL IN TIME

The Boeing 777 cuts its way through the night and Danny settles back to enjoy the experience. As a small child he travelled tens of thousands of miles, but most of them were spent sitting high up front in one of the Mysterium's dark-blue lorries, or alongside Dad in the van as they cruised down yet another long European motorway. He was too young to remember the US tour and can only just recall South America in fragments, so long-haul flight is a novelty.

I've missed the travelling, he thinks. New sights, new sounds. That feeling you get as you come into a new city. New people. The sky map on his monitor shows the familiar cities of Western Europe slowly being replaced by places he has never seen in Russia.

'Feels a bit odd, I expect,' Laura says. 'Finally making this journey, I mean . . . You must be thinking about your mum?'

'Sort of.'

'Dad too, I guess.'

He bites his lip. The truth is he doesn't know what to think. Doesn't *even* know if he wants to think about it or not.

Maybe Hong Kong will help, he thinks, repeating the thought like a mantra. Even if it brings up the painful stuff. Mum always talked longingly about the food, the weather. The temples and the lush hills and countryside. But when he pressed her – and tried to find out more about her past life there – she would clam tight and change the subject. And when, in response to his persistent questions, she promised to take him there one day, it always had the feeling of 'one day' that would never come.

'I wish I remembered more Cantonese. Mum used to speak a bit, but in the end we stuck to English.'

'Your dad was always a terrible linguist,' Laura says. 'One thing he couldn't do! Maybe some of it will come back to you. Anyway, most people who deal with tourists still speak English. Not that long since we rented the place from the Chinese, after all!'

'Can you tell me about the story you're doing?'

'Oh, don't worry about that, Danny boy,' Laura says brightly. Slightly too brightly. 'Just have a good time with Zamora. Eat noodles. Leave the bad guys to me.'

'It feels like you're not telling me things, Aunt Laura.'

'Honestly not, Danny. Scouts honour.'

'I'm not a little kid any more,' he says, cutting her short. 'There's something you're not saying. About the trip.'

It comes out sharper than he intends. But it's frustrating the way silence descends whenever he asks the tricky questions. About his parents' deaths, for example. People were kind and supportive, of course – Laura especially – and he appreciated that. It helped him cope with the shock, cope with how much he missed Dad's deep voice describing the world and the wonders in it, missed Mum's quick smile, steadfast optimism. Their love. He can just about cope with that. Most days.

And he can generally push from his mind the wreck of their trailer, the deathly hush that hung over the Mysterium encampment, the white-sheeted stretchers. He can cope with all that.

Just about.

But he can't cope with the fact that nobody, not even Laura, ever seems to want to answer the 'difficult' questions directly.

'I'm growing up, Aunt Laura. I can deal with stuff.'

'I suppose you are, Danny. Fair point.' She glances around the cabin, then drops her voice. 'Well, this lot are a really nasty Triad gang.'

'Triad?'

'Organized criminal gangs. Centuries old. Bit like the Mafia with a big code of honour and secrecy. This lot are called the Black Dragon. A bunch of upstarts forcing their way into the Chinese underworld. And they're reaching out to gangs back home in Britain. I want to get up close and personal – and show how dangerous they are. Not glamorous. Just thugs.'

'What do they do?'

'Most of these gangs stick to drugs, pornography, human trafficking. But this lot have their fingers in a lot of pies. Getting into kidnapping. People are paying up because they realize the Dragon means business.'

'How?'

Laura taps her fingers on the tray table. 'They send the relatives locks of hair, with a warning to pay up fast. If they don't, they get something else.'

'Like what?'

'A box of steamed dim sum, wrapped up like a gift . . . and in one of the dumplings there will be the victim's little finger. Maybe two.'

Laura laughs apologetically. 'Like I say, Danny,

"fingers in a lot of pies". Just experimenting with a tagline. They use boltcutters, I believe.'

'How would you know whose finger it was?'

Laura waggles her little finger in front of his face. 'You'd recognize this little piggy wouldn't you?'

Danny's stomach tightens, a brief image in his head of Laura's lively finger severed and bloody on a white plate. He pulls a face. 'And how do you get close to them? The Black Dragon?'

'Curiosity killed the cat. Don't you know that?'

'Doesn't seem to stop you.'

'This cat's got a lot of lives left, Danny boy.'

'Mum always used to say that . . . if something went wrong—'

'And anyway,' Laura adds quickly, 'I've got an inside source in the Hong Kong Police. Organized Crime and Triad Bureau. Going to meet him tomorrow. Decent guy, not like some of them, bent as old nails.'

A stewardess is working a trolley down the aisle, pulling level with them.

'We've got English or Chinese for you today, young man,' the stewardess says. 'Which do you feel like? Sausage and mash, or a lovely selection of dim sum . . .'

'Sausage and mash,' Danny says quickly, the image

of Laura's severed finger still sharp in his head. But then he changes his mind. 'No. I'll have the dim sum. Thanks.'

'Good choice,' Laura says. 'After all, at least a part of you is going home!'

After dinner he lifts the blind on the porthole and stares out into the dark. Laura is rattling away on her laptop, humming like she does when working a story. Dad would have been able to read so much in her eyes from micro-muscles you can't voluntarily control, which betray memory, emotion. Or by the exact way she's set her shoulders. Danny knows how it's done in theory, but hasn't enough experience to be sure of anything. I'll just have to wait and see, he thinks.

As the engines pulse, he watches ice crystals form in the glazing of the window and slowly he drifts into a reverie: not quite awake, not quite asleep, eyes half closing. He slips in time, memories playing again in vivid colour. When his guard is down they come back, unbidden – in bits and pieces . . .

Now, in his mind's eye, he's there. He's at the Mysterium again. Kaleidoscopic images well up into consciousness: he sees the Aerialisques tumbling on their red silk ropes from high in the hemisphere, finishing their burlesque-like act to a chorus of wolf whistles, applause, cheering.

Half asleep, he drifts with the memory and sees the bearded electric guitarist, the pretty tattooed cellist, climb to their places high in the rigging and start the hypnotic riffs that signal Dad's great new escapology routine. The amplified music throbs around the arena.

. . . And there's Mum watching from the performers' entrance, peeking between the curtains, her bright-green eyes fixed on Dad as he is fastened into the straitjacket and chains. She doesn't normally watch, but this is a first performance. She can't help herself. Maybe more tension in her face than normal.

And there, bright in the spotlight, Danny sees the water torture cell waiting for its prisoner. Every detail clear, as if he is still standing in front of it. A re-invention of Houdini's famous escape: a glass tank – brimful of water – the size of a small lift. Its wooden frame is freshly painted red, the water inside reflecting the strobing lights, a projected image of Houdini's own garish publicity poster.

And then Dad's feet are fastened into the ugly-looking stocks and hoisted up above his head by the winch. He dangles upside down at the end of the chain, smiling out over the expectant faces of the crowd, spotlight bright on his powerful figure, over the head of Zamora, who waits, axe poised 'just in case' for dramatic effect. But there will be no need to use it. Nothing ever goes wrong for Dad.

The straitjacket and padlocks confine his arms tightly to his side as he hovers for a moment in the air. And then down he goes, *kerploof*, head first into the water . . .

Bubbles stream from his mouth and nose as he twists and writhes in the tank. Time runs through the animated hourglass now projected on the tank. The music picks up, insistent. Dad's hair waves like seaweed in the churning water, face a mixture of concentration and effort. Two minutes left to free himself, or he will drown.

The tank is visibly shaking as he puts all of his effort into the escape, body flexing and straightening as he usually does to start to loosen the bonds. The water laps over the top, running down the glass, distorting his figure.

But something's wrong: it's all taking far too long. He's normally out of the first of the cuffs already. Close up, his father's face shows anxiety. Fear even . . . The stopwatch is ticking away in Danny's hand. Come on, Dad. Come on—

* * *

'Hey, Danny!'

Laura taps him on the shoulder, snapping him back to the present, the engine roar. 'If you're going to sleep then use a cushion and a blanket and make the best of it.'

He turns to look at her drowsily. Something has been prompted by the waking dream.

'Aunt Laura. Did you ever see the Water Torture Escape. In rehearsal, I mean?'

'I was always too busy.' She sighs.

'There's something weird about it. I mean, weird how it went wrong. And then the fire so soon after—'

'Danny, we've been over that—'

'You said we could see about looking into it again.'

'The police did a thorough job. Death by accidental causes.'

'But Mum and Dad were always so careful—'

'*You* saw the report. I'm sure it was kosher. Accidents happen.'

There it is again. No one ever wanted to listen, and when he persisted last year, a psychologist patiently explained that the doubts were all to do with shock – the difficulty in believing that someone was gone. That something as stupid as a cooking fire could take the lives of people who looked death in the face and cheated it on a daily basis.

'It doesn't make sense. Two things going so wrong in a week.'

Laura sighs. 'Life just sometimes has a habit of wrong-footing us, Daniel. God only knows that's happened to me enough. We don't know what's coming round the corner. Good or bad.'

'But Dad always said—'

'Your dad didn't know everything, Danny. He liked to think he did. I'm sorry, but we're all of us groping in the dark sometimes.'

He nods, but isn't convinced. One failed escape in the week, maybe. But not two. It doesn't feel right – never has done.

He stares out into the night again. Nothing to be seen of the unknown lands slipping by far below.

'Get some sleep now, Danny.'

But when he does eventually drift off, his dreams are dark and disturbed. Full of the rush and chaos of water closing over his head.

5 HOW NOT TO JUDGE BY APPEARANCES

Sunlight streams through the windows of the sprawling Hong Kong International. Lushly wooded hills roll in the distance, their unfamiliar shapes pricking his excitement, the misgivings of the night before replaced by a surge of anticipation at finally seeing Hong Kong. And of being reunited with Zamora.

There's a thick scrum at the arrivals gate, but it's not exactly hard to spot the dwarf. A good deal shorter than the rest, he nevertheless stands out at the barrier, raised up on tiptoe, his trademark bowler hat perched at a jaunty angle. One hand reaches up to smooth his moustache. Then he spots Danny and a broad smile breaks across his face as he bustles forward to greet them, arms working busily, head held high.

'There you are, there you are, Mister Danny. Miss Laura!' He gives Danny a powerful hug, lifting him clean off the ground. 'You've blooming well overtaken me. I knew it. Oh well. Had to happen.'

'It's been so long—' Danny says, recovering from the dwarf's grip. He wants to say more, but can't find the words.

'No problem for us, Mister Danny. No *problema*! Old friends can cope with time, you know. We're here now. That's all that matters.' He play-punches his young friend on the shoulder.

'How's the hotel?' Laura says.

'Bit too posh. Made me put a shirt over my lovely pictures.' The dwarf flexes his biceps and the mermaids and tigers inked there jump and twist. 'But otherwise like you asked. Anonymous. Central.'

'Let's get moving then, shall we, boys?' Laura says.

Zamora takes the trolley and starts to shove it through the crowds, throwing words back over his shoulder. 'We'll have a good time, eh, Mister Danny? Catch up, talk about the old days . . . EAT, for God's sake. You know what they say – food is an important part of a balanced diet! How's the magic?'

Danny smiles. 'I'll show you the jumping man. I've almost got it.' The long year and a half since that snowy Berlin day feels like it's melting into nothing.

'Never show a trick till you're absolutely sure of him,' Zamora says. 'Hey! Tell me I've grown!'

It's an old joke. 'You've grown, Major.'

'Four foot four! Not bad for an achondroplasic, *no*? Has Laura been telling you about the mess she's—'

'Found a driver yet?' Laura cuts quickly across him. 'I need to hit the ground running.'

Danny spots that easily enough. Somewhere Laura didn't want to go.

'What mess?'

'Oh,' Laura says, 'just too much to do and not enough time. As usual. How about this driver?'

Zamora changes tack smoothly. 'Oh yes. Nice man. He's here somewhere.' He lifts himself on the trolley handles, peering over the crowds. 'There he is. Mr Kwan!'

A short, rotund man – not much taller than the Major himself – steps forward and takes hold of a case.

'Pleased to meet you,' he says, nodding at all three, squinting through thick round glasses. He reminds Danny of the barn owl that used to greet visitors at the Mysterium's entrance. It always looked confused to find itself there – and took the first opportunity it got to escape into a dark Spanish night. That had pleased Danny – and the resemblance makes him warm to Kwan.

'This way, please,' the taxi driver says, leading them

through the revolving doors. It feels to Danny as if they've walked into a solid wall of muggy air and hot sun slaps him on the back of the neck. The change of atmosphere, from grey lifeless Ballstone to the heat of this morning – Cantonese sing-songing all around them – is stirring something deep inside. Genetic memory maybe? He opens up his senses, trying to take it all in.

Kwan's red and white taxi is waiting for them, sunlight bouncing off dented bodywork. An advert for teeth whitening is plastered to the driver's door. It looks as though someone's taken a sledgehammer repeatedly to that side of the car, and Laura raises an eyebrow as Kwan starts banging cases into the boot.

'Don't judge by appearances,' Zamora whispers. 'Your brother always told me that, Miss Laura.'

'As long as he can actually drive the damn thing.'

'Remember what Shakespeare said, Miss Laura. "All that glitters is not gold." And vice versa. Mr Kwan's a good one. Picked him third off the rank, just like you said.'

'Point taken.'

'And don't I know what it is to be misjudged,' Zamora mutters.

Danny is looking around, savouring the heat, watching travellers pulse in and out of the terminal building. I'm ready for this, he thinks. It feels right to be here.

Close by, a tall man is lounging against a lamppost, mobile phone casually held to his ear. The morning sun falls on his spotless white linen suit. Although seemingly immersed in his call, he casts a quick glance at them.

Despite the throng of new images coming at him, it registers with Danny. There's nothing new about people staring at Zamora, of course. The Major turns heads wherever he goes – and grumbles about it on a bad day – but there's something about the spark in the man's gaze that holds Danny's attention for a second or two. It just doesn't match the relaxed posture of the rest of his body. 'Pay attention when things don't fit,' Dad always said. 'Be interested in the details.'

But then the man claps his phone shut, shoves it in a pocket and ambles off towards the terminal doors. As if he has all the time in the world.

'Come on,' Zamora says, clambering into the rear seat of Kwan's cab. 'Your aunt's in a blooming hurry. As usual. And I'm hungry.'

Kwan revs the taxi and they pull away towards the expressway.

'Damn sight better arriving here than the old airport,' Zamora says. 'Safer too!'

Danny looks back at the terminal building – and sees the man in the suit dart back across the tarmac, summoning the next taxi on the rank with a flick of his fingers. He moves with precision, ducking his long, thin head as he jumps into the back seat – glancing in their direction as he goes.

'My God, it was scary in a crosswind,' the dwarf continues. 'Planes sliding sideways . . .'

But Danny's not listening. His curiosity has been roused by the actions of the white-suited man and he looks around again, trying to pick out the other taxi. There it is. Close behind.

It follows them across a couple of intersections and then down the ramp onto the North Lantau Highway. Most taxis from the airport would be going this way, of course. Then again, the man has no baggage, and he was in a hurry to grab a taxi as soon as they left the rank. Bit odd.

Kwan wipes his forehead with a red handkerchief, urging the car onwards. They climb an elegant suspension bridge, cables webbed against the sky.

Zamora taps Danny on the shoulder, dragging his attention from the following cab

'Take a look, Danny.'

All of Hong Kong and its harbour is spread out before them in one breathtaking sweep. Boats plough slow white furrows on the water. Green hills rise and fall and rise again, cradling the bay. Everywhere the thrust of skyscrapers, towers of glass and steel vertical at the water's edge, catching the light.

'One of the most densely populated places on Earth,' Laura says. 'That's why everyone builds upwards. Up and up.'

'And me with my vertigo,' says Zamora, grimacing. '*Ay caramba!*'

The expressway snakes through flyovers and sprawling intersections. Danny's eyes drinking in the approaching city. Signs flashing by in a clutter of Chinese characters, coded messages that feel as though they should be decipherable, but are beyond reach.

'It's strange to think of Mum growing up here,' Danny says, watching the city grow around them, the towering blocks swallowing them up.

'How do you mean, Danny boy?' Laura asks.

'I mean, it's like there's a whole life she had here that I don't really know.'

'Perhaps you'll get a better feel for it . . .'

Danny smiles. 'I'm glad I've come.'

'Good. I'm sure it was the right thing to do.'

Kwan pilots them surely enough through the hustling traffic and then down a ramp into the cross-harbour tunnel to Hong Kong Island itself.

Danny turns round to squint through the rear window. Is that taxi still following us? he wonders. No fewer than twenty other virtually identical red and white cabs crowd behind them. No chance of picking it out. Maybe he was mistaken anyway.

He keeps looking for a long time before finally twisting back again.

Zamora glances at him. Not hard to see the mixture of anxiety, excitement, grief playing there. Going to be a bit of a balancing act, the dwarf thinks. We need to lift the boy's spirits.

But we need to keep our eyes open too. Just in case.

6 HOW TO TRUST YOUR INSTINCTS

They turn along the waterfront. The traffic has snarled, bumper to bumper. People nudge to change lanes. Horns blaring.

It makes him think of the Khaos Klowns doing their Demolition Derby routine – souped-up bumper cars ramming across the arena, colliding in flame and smoke as the band thumped out a fuzzed guitar riff. One by one the Aerialisques came dropping from out of the air on their bungee cords, plucking the drivers from their dodgems – the Klowns suddenly sprouting angel wings as they ascended in the girls' arms – and calm slowly returned to the arena. He finds himself smiling. Almost as if he chose to have that memory . . .

Laura claps her hands, breaking the spell. 'Attention in the back, please. I'm going to get Mr Kwan to drop you and the bags at the Pearl. I've got to go and meet Detective Tan, my contact.' She scribbles on a business card and hands it to Danny. 'This is a restaurant in Mong Kok. Across the harbour in Kowloon. Take the Star Ferry and meet me there. 8 p.m. sharp.'

They lurch onto the forecourt of the Pearl Hotel, a great slab of glass commanding Victoria Harbour. The taxi backfires as Kwan brings it to a stop, and Danny looks back at the puff of smoke from the exhaust.

Through it he sees White Suit again.

The other taxi, presumably the same one from the airport, has pulled up some way back and the tall, thin man is on the pavement, chatting to his driver through the window. Again, as casual as you like. But then he glances – for a fraction of a second – straight in Danny's direction, before a green tram trundles past, obliterating him from view.

A coincidence?

Danny nudges Zamora. 'I'm not sure, but I think we're being followed. Don't look round too quickly, but a tall man, white suit.'

'Come off it, Mister Danny!'

'I'm sure he was at the airport. And now he's here.'

'Then he's probably staying at the same hotel.'

Kwan is piling cases onto the pavement and a bellhop starts loading them onto a trolley. 'Here, let me help, young man,' Zamora says, swinging out of the cab and effortlessly picking up the two biggest. 'Our fault for bringing so much.'

Laura ruffles Danny's quiff.

'Aunt Laura—'

'No time now. I just need to speed-freshen.' She takes perfume from her bag and sprays her wrist liberally. He's never really liked its cloying smell and he wrinkles his nose. Laura looks into Danny's eyes – holding his gaze for a moment. 'Do what the Major says. At all times. Understand?'

'But—'

'It'll have to wait!'

Reluctantly Danny gets out of the taxi.

Laura taps Kwan on the shoulder. He crunches the gears hard and sends the car lurching into an almost non-existent gap between the cars and a tram. In seconds they're gone.

Danny turns round to check for White Suit. The man's still there by his taxi and seems to hesitate for a moment, throwing another glance at Danny – right at him – before snapping back into his own cab. Kwan's car is lost in the traffic ahead, but you can tell where it is by the exhaust coughing from its tailpipe. White Suit points after it, and his own taxi darts forward. It clips a delivery van a glancing blow and is away down

Connaught Road, to a fanfare of protesting horns.

Danny watches it for a moment before turning to Zamora, eyebrows raised.

'You see?'

'I dunno, Mister Danny. Crazy place.'

'Didn't you see him?'

'Just some josser in a hurry,' Zamora says. 'Like always. Like your aunt. Not like us circus folk.'

He shakes his head and goes in through the revolving doors, keeping his eyes lowered. 'Crazy.'

Maybe this White Suit business is nothing, Danny thinks. Maybe Laura did change her plans at the last minute. Maybe she has told me everything she knows. And yet, deep down, he knows that's wrong. In the circus you were taught to trust that sixth sense, that survival instinct. Somewhere – quietly at the back of your mind – it might be whispering its warning.

And it might just save your life.

7 HOW TO CATCH A FURTIVE DWARF

The Pearl Hotel may be anonymous but it is certainly grand.

Potted palms and acres of marble. Mirrors and polished chrome reflect the uniformed bellhops, while the wealthy men and women lounging around look bored and irritable.

Danny watches Zamora chatting to the receptionist, the dwarf's infectious laughter punctuating their conversation. The Major's solid presence is reassuring, and, despite the questions ticking away in his mind, Danny decides to let things lie. At least for now. Zamora turns away from the desk and comes back over, scratching his head.

'We're on the seventh floor! Could be worse. Heightwise, I mean!'

'How'd you ever manage in the circus, Major?'

'It's OK if I'm doing something. Like riding the

wall. And the cannonball thing was always over so quickly I didn't realize how blinking high I went. Until I saw it on video one day.'

The dwarf grimaces, shoulders Danny's bag along with his own and leads the way to the lifts. Danny checks over his shoulder as they go, the sudden urgency of White Suit's actions out on the road still dogging his thoughts.

In room 712 a floor-to-ceiling window reveals a dramatic panorama of the harbour, the sprawl of Kowloon on the far side, clouds boiling up over the hills and China beyond. Zamora approaches the window and peers at the sky uncertainly.

'What shall we do first, Mister Danny? How about showing me this jumping man of yours?'

'OK. I'll find my cards.'

'Good. Then we'll see about—'

Zamora stops mid-sentence, his head cocked on one side, as if listening to something. Nothing obvious to be heard above the hum of the air con, but the lines on the dwarf's brow deepen.

'Tell you what. How about you practise a couple of times? I'm just going to have a quick word with the concierge. Won't be a moment.'

It's Danny's turn to frown now. A distinct note of tension has crept into Zamora's voice.

'I'll do our secret knock when I'm back. Like the old days, *no*?'

Puzzled, Danny goes to sit by the window, riffling the cards through his fingers, watching Zamora move stealthily towards their door. The dwarf pauses there for a moment, again listening hard, and then slips out of the room. Danny hears him muttering away in Spanish under his breath – and then the door snicks shut.

Weird. There's definitely something up, and yet again things are being kept from him. He drops the cards back into his pocket and moves silently across the room, pausing by the door, and – yes – there's a faint sound to be heard. Like someone breathing in a laboured way, a dry rasping sound. OK then, so let's see what's going on.

He whips the door open and catches Zamora crouched on the floor, caught in the act – of what? The dwarf half falls into the room, and then looks up at Danny. Something guilty in that glance.

There's a paper tissue in his hand, and, low down on the polished wooden door, a smudge of what looks like chalk.

'Some kid must have been playing silly buggers,' the dwarf says.

But what remains of the graffiti grips Danny's attention. There's two and a half tiny rows of dots neatly done right at the base of the door. Above that they smudge into a chalky cloud.

'Think I'm only making it worse,' Zamora says, rubbing away again at the pattern.

Something familiar about the dots, Danny thinks, even as the last of them disappear. I've seen something like it. Recently.

He closes his eyes. Something here in Hong Kong? No, before that. How many dots in the row? Six or so? At school, after the explosion. He remembers that charred paper he stuffed into his back pocket.

'Major,' Danny says. 'I saw a pattern like that at school last week. It was a square, made of dots. Seven by seven, I think. Was that the same?'

The strongman stops dead, sucking a breath in through his teeth. He feigns nonchalance – the kind of thing he forced each time he lowered himself down the barrel of the spring-loaded cannon.

'Seven by seven, you say? At school?'

'Yes. After the explosion.'

'Did you tell Miss Laura about it?'

'No. I forgot about it. Until just now.'

Zamora's on his feet, stuffing the hankie into his pocket and striding towards the phone on the desk. 'Think I'll just give her a quick ring.'

'What does it mean?'

'Hmm,' Zamora grunts. 'What?'

'That pattern.'

The dwarf puffs out his cheeks, listening expectantly. He shakes his head.

'Switched off.'

'And the man in the white suit. The one following us?'

'*No hay problema*. But do you know what, Mister Danny? I'm not so keen on this room after all. Let's see if we can't get it changed.'

'Answer me!'

But Zamora just shakes his head and reaches for the phone.

There were two kinds of silence that used to fall in the circus trailer after a long day on the road, or after a performance.

There was the easy one: when Mum and Dad would potter around, removing their stage make-up, preparing a meal on the little stove. Nothing to be said, just the peace that comes after rewarding effort. A day gone well.

But then there was – occasionally – the strained one: the uncomfortable silence when something was going unsaid. A rare, unvoiced disagreement, a strain in the connection between them. Something fragile. First Dad, then Mum would glance at him, then look away again, and the air in the trailer seemed heavier. There were a lot more of those silences on that final tour as they ticked off the cities and headed towards Berlin. Destiny. Cold weather locked around the Mysterium, somehow making the unfathomable hush all the more glacial.

Now, in a new hotel room five floors higher, a silence as heavy as any of those has descended. From time to time, Zamora tries Laura's mobile, the lines furrowing deeper on his forehead, and then goes to gaze again at the harbour, his vertigo forgotten.

Eventually after one last try he bangs the phone back on the desk. 'Now it's damn well gone to unobtainable. What does that mean? She's always gabbing on the thing. Or Twittering or whatever it's called.'

He coughs and turns round, staring hard at the floor. 'We'll see her soon enough.' Then tries to lighten the mood. 'Well then, Mister Danny. How's school? Made many friends?'

'They think circuses are for little kids.'

'Goes to show how much these jossers know. Remember the Khaos Klowns, for God's sake. They even gave me the willies. And the Aerialisques? Hot stuff . . . *no?*' He laughs, but his heart's not in it.

Danny is fidgeting the cards between his fingers again. I always thought Zamora would tell me everything, he thinks. Never treated me like a little kid. Not even when I was tiny.

Frustrated, he picks the top card from the deck, and with a sharp snap of index and middle fingers, sends it hissing through the air. It strikes the desk lamp on the far side of the room with a clunk. Bullseye.

'Did old Blanco teach you that?' Zamora says.

'Yep.'

'Best knifethrower I ever saw.'

Danny goes over to Zamora at the window. Purple and black clouds are packing the horizon, bruising the sky. His fingers keep fiddling the deck anxiously – and suddenly it slips and he's fumbled all the cards to the floor. He turns to face Zamora.

'Do you know what this diagram is . . . the dots?'

'Oh well,' Zamora says, flapping his arms in

discomfort. 'Probably nothing.'

He turns away, trying to bring the subject to a close – and silence falls again. Suddenly it's not the reunion Danny has hoped for.

'So why change our room then? Why the rush to get Laura—'

'Damn it all, I'm sure there is nothing to worry about,' Zamora snaps, an edge to his voice that brings Danny up short.

'Sorry. Just tired,' the dwarf says, flopping back on the bed, closing his eyes. 'Let's recharge a bit before dinner.'

In seconds, just like the old days when they had arrived in some new city and finished the pitching of the encampment, he's fast asleep, leaving Danny to stare out at the harbour.

He eyes the clouds, mulling over the day and its developments. There's a storm gathering. You can feel it charging the air.

A few hours later they're on the deck of the Star Ferry as it churns the harbour towards Kowloon. Darkness has fallen but it's still very warm, clouds pressing down on the city and the South China Sea, the sweat prickling Danny's neck and forehead. Dazzling neon splashes on the buildings and skyscrapers rake in vertical stripes against the night.

But Danny is looking down at the black water, his head bowed. Zamora goes to join him at the rail and stands there for a moment before putting a hand on his shoulder.

Further back in the crowd, tucked under the shadow of the wheelhouse, White Suit stands impassively, his body alert, eyes for nothing but Danny and his stocky companion. Then he reaches into his pocket, resting his hand on something hidden from sight, his face a mask.

8 HOW TO BLEND INTO A CROWD

Kowloon breaks around them. Sleek downtown giving way to the vibrant hustle of Mong Kok. The pavements are rammed, spilling over onto the street, a barrage of jostling crowds, restaurant touts. Buses shudder past trailed by the buzz of scooters. Cafés and street stalls spill aromas on the night air, competing with the punch of diesel fumes. Chinese characters pulse overhead, distant sirens and loudspeakers filling the air with Chinese pop and adverts. The energy of it all lifts Danny's spirits.

'Hold on to your hat,' Zamora says. 'Lively, no?'

He unfolds a map and glances at the address on Laura's card. '*Vamos*. This way.'

The dwarf's powerful shoulders push through the crowds, moving easily, without tension. Maybe there really is nothing to fear. Nevertheless Danny's eyes flick across the crowds as they go. If only he knew what to look out for. At least White Suit will stick out if he's anywhere near.

They move deeper into the frenetic night city, Zamora chatting away, ignoring the touts trying to grab their attention.

'So I was touring with the Micro last year and guess what? I bumped into old Jimmy Torrini. Still doing his Dr Oblivion routine, can you believe that? But he's punked it up a bit. Didn't seem too pleased to see me!'

There's a flicker in a gap between the buildings and then the first long growl of thunder comes rolling down from the hills.

'Dad always said he was OK. Even when Rosa fired him.'

'Maybe so. Your dad was a good judge, after all. Picked me as a brainbox when all people ever saw were the muscles! This way.'

As Danny and Zamora turn a corner another lightning flash stutters across the sky. It freeze-frames Laura, standing in the middle of the street, her camcorder hanging by her side with the boom mic strapped to it and a bright smile stamped on her face.

'Storm a'coming! Hurry up!'

Zamora sighs. 'Your stupid phone's not working.'

'Someone bloody nicked it off a café table. I'll sort it tomorrow. Hungry?'

'I could eat the whole menu. But I just need a quick word.'

'Just a minute, Major.'

Laura pulls them into the hubbub of The Golden Bat restaurant. 'Bit theme park, I'm afraid, but they say the won ton here's the real deal. Hey, you were right about Kwan, Major Zee. He was a rock. All afternoon.'

The air is laden with soy sauce and spice. Danny's gaze takes in the red lanterns, curling dragons, explosive black calligraphy on the walls as Laura leads them to a table on a platform at the back. Nearby, tropical fish stir colour into the water of a huge aquarium.

'Best table in the house, boys. Want you to meet a couple of people.'

A Chinese man in a pinstripe suit is already seated there, his face set in stone, dark and thoughtful. He nods almost imperceptibly in greeting. Not the kind of face you could ever hope to read, Danny thinks. He's giving nothing away – except for the fact that he doesn't want to give anything away.

Next to him is a young girl. Her almond-shaped face is framed by the long black hair that falls to the shoulders of her slim-fitting leather jacket. Thirteen, fourteen? It's hard to tell. Something knowing in her quick, dark eyes, maybe something a little bit hard.

She glances at Danny. For a second a smile lights her face – and then she looks away at the fishtank. That's easy to read. She was trying to hide her reaction. Defensive maybe? Wants the world to see a tough-girl exterior.

'Welcome,' the man says. 'I'm Charlie Chow. This is my daughter, Sing Sing.'

The girl's face flashes. 'Adopted!' she corrects. Her eyes flit back to Danny, seeking him out. For a moment their eyes lock again, and then her gaze slips to the Mysterium tour shirt – its bleached skull, staring vacant eye sockets, fragile butterflies, glowing letters. She nods to herself. Approval? As if she's ticking things off from a checklist.

'I'm Danny,' he says, holding out his hand. Sing Sing looks at it, feigning a studied boredom now – then slowly reaches out to shake. When their hands make contact, he is surprised to find her palm and fingers are hard and calloused. She withdraws her hand quickly, again as if not wanting to disclose too much. She's interesting, Danny thinks. A lot going on under the surface.

Laura's getting to her feet.

'We've just got to do a quick piece in the street, before Mister Chow has to be off.'

'Excuse us,' Chow says. 'Anything you want is on the house.'

'But, Miss Laura—'

'Two shakes, Major.' Laura's already leading Chow towards the street. 'Tell you something, though, boys,' she calls over her shoulder. 'Detective Tan has gone on "sick leave". No one can reach him. If you can believe *that*!'

'Your aunt says you do magic tricks?' Sing Sing says abruptly. 'So, you any damn good?' There's something challenging in her voice. Mocking even – go on, impress me, it says, her eyes underlining that challenge.

'I'm OK,' Danny says.

'I do some tricks too.'

'Cards and stuff like that?' Danny says, intrigued.

'Bit like that.'

Her mobile trills. She hesitates a moment and then looks right into his odd-coloured eyes. 'So. You as good as your dad then?' She holds up both hands, wrists tight together, miming the restraint of handcuffs, that same smile. Teasing. Before he can answer, she flips open her mobile and starts to talk under her breath in rapid Cantonese.

Emotion kicks through Danny's system. Excitement at the mention of Dad, but confusion too. As if the girl has the advantage. What does she know about Dad? She glances back at Danny now, her eyes afire in the dark interior of the Bat, then gets to her feet and goes to stand on the other side of the aquarium, mobile pressed to her ear. Listening hard now.

He watches her intently, trying to read her expression, but the tank distorts everything, smudging her features. Something strained in her shoulders, as if she's waiting for something to happen. The fish churn the water in between, blurring his view. Danny watches them for a moment, distracted – that uncomfortable memory again of Dad desperately struggling in the water torture cell.

'What do you think five-snake stew tastes like?' the Major says, eyeing the menu. 'And how's your aunt doing?'

From where they sit, there's a good view back through the open front of the restaurant to the street outside. Laura's got Chow in her camcorder sights, her voice swallowed by the restaurant noise.

Suddenly Danny stiffens and the mention of Dad – his curiosity about Sing Sing – are forgotten. 'Major!'

White Suit is going past at speed, brushing Laura's shoulder, moving with that same long stride. Precise, controlled. Out of sight in a moment.

The thunder detonates overhead, making the diners around them jump.

'*Madre mia!*' Zamora says. 'I'll blend in and try and follow him.'

Danny is just thinking how hard it will be for a tattooed dwarf strongman to blend in to a Kowloon evening, when all hell breaks loose.

A motorbike comes buzzing down the street. Then another.

They skid to a stop right next to Laura and Chow, one of the riders barking out Cantonese. Simultaneously a black BMW reverses fast up the street from the other direction, gears whining in protest. Laura is surrounded by six or so young men, grabbing the camera, pushing Chow to the ground, all shouting at once.

Two of them are brandishing meat cleavers – big ones – and the light glints off their blades as the men raise them threateningly over their heads.

Zamora and Danny are already on their way to help, moving towards the door. But now two other men push back their chairs and get to their feet, blocking the way. The first of them pulls a long knife out from his sleeve.

The other is gaunt faced, sharply dressed in a

well-cut suit, his hair slicked back in a pony tail. He makes a move for his jacket pocket, shouting at them.

Danny tries to dodge round them, but the first man has him by the shoulders and shoves him forcefully back against a pillar. The knife flashes wildly. Danny ducks and the blade strikes a glancing blow off the plasterwork.

From outside you can hear Laura giving as good as she gets: 'Let go of ME! I have friends in the police!'

Major Zamora's eyes have gone dark. No one messes with Mister Danny. No way.

'I kill him, Danny,' he shouts. 'I kill him for you now!' He grabs hold of a chair and swings it hard at the knifeman, breaking it over his head with a splintering of wood, sending him slumping to the ground, blood bright on his temple. Pony Tail's jaw slackens, astonished, but he has no time to react before Zamora is on him, swinging the remains of the chair for all he's worth.

'Come on then, *amigo!*'

A loud gunshot cracks through the confusion, but the dwarf keeps going unchecked. He grabs hold of Pony Tail and sends him flying full tilt, backwards across the restaurant, somersaulting over a table, slamming into the aquarium with a sickening crack. His eyes close and he crumples.

Crazy-paving cracks spread across the tank's surface – the world seems to freeze – and then the whole thing shatters, sending glass and water cascading across the floor, fish flop-flipping in the torrent, gulping at the air.

Danny scrambles between the overturned chairs and out onto the street towards where Laura is being bundled into the waiting car. She twists her head in desperation, catching one of the thugs a decent right hook, and manages to lean out.

'RED notebook, Danny! RED—'

The hoodlums pile in after her and slam the door shut, and then the BMW's tyres are burning the tarmac and it's away down the street like a startled animal.

Danny gives chase, but then has to throw himself out of the way as one of the motorbikes comes straight at him from behind. He jumps and rolls, coming back onto his feet in one movement.

Zamora stumbles out of the restaurant waving half a bloodied chair leg, glaring at the two remaining thugs. They both hesitate, then leap onto the second motorbike and are gone, leaving nothing but exhaust.

Of Mister Chow there is no sign.

'*Caramba!*' Zamora says. 'Someone call the blasted police . . .'

Danny watches the BMW cornering hard. It clips a bollard, striking a bright spark against the night. Laura's face framed for a moment in its back window. Then it's gone.

Zamora glares after them, breathing hard. 'Don't worry, Danny. It'll be OK. The police will sort it out. At least we've got a couple of them here. Scumbags.'

Danny looks at him, eyes blazing, both the green and the brown dotted with fire.

'It's my fault,' he says.

'Don't be daft, Danny.'

But guilt is reaching surely out to tighten its grip.

'It's my fault,' he repeats.

It starts to rain, heavy drops falling one by one at first, kicking up the dust on the street, a hesitant rhythm tapping at the car roofs. It gathers pace. And then the clouds burst apart.

The thunder keeps prowling overhead as they wait for the police, and the rain thickens. But still Danny doesn't move.

A growing sense of desperation has taken hold of his legs, his breathing.

He recognizes that sensation – it's the same one that set in after the fire. Instead of 'running away' that night – he had got no further than the far side of the encampment and bedded down in the prop store – he should have been with Mum and Dad. Then maybe he would have smelled the smoke and woken everyone and saved the day. Or put the first flames out. Or maybe it's just the typical guilt of a survivor: I should have been there. After Berlin – after the initial shock had subsided – it had held him tight for weeks, months. Stopped him from acting, from chasing down the truth about those last few weeks in the Mysterium. Kept him lying on his bed, worrying away at the vague emotion.

But *this* guilt is more concrete.

He ticks the items off in his mind. I knew about the dots. I knew White Suit was following us. I should have made Laura listen, dammit.

Danny takes a breath – feels the ground firm beneath his feet – loosens his shoulders, softens his knees. A qigong move that Blanco taught him. This time he won't let the guilt take him prisoner. He won't let it get the better of him.

Zamora comes to stand beside him in the downpour. 'I'm going to sort this out, Major.'

'One step at a time now, Danny. Let's start with the police . . .'

The rain batters down, clearing his head. Not just from the jet lag and the tiredness of the journey, but from that long hibernation of the last sixteen months. Waking up. A process that began with the explosion is continuing now under the full force of the storm. He looks up and lets the drops sting his face, slapping his skin into tingling life. Determination growing, he shakes the water from his head.

'I'm going to find her, Major.'

The dwarf looks hesitant.

'Are you with me?'

'Of course, Mister Danny. Every step of the way. But let's get out of this monsoon. And talk to the police, *no*?'

'What happened to Sing Sing? And Mister Chow?'

In all the chaos it seems they have vanished into the night. Even with the shock of the kidnap and fight buzzing his veins, Danny feels dismayed at that. What did the girl know about Dad? Why does it feel like he's met Sing Sing before? And what has happened to her?

They go back into the Golden Bat and survey the damage. Waiters are escorting diners out through the broken glass and upturned furniture, whilst two chefs mount a rescue operation for the fish, scooping the frantically twitching survivors into a plastic bucket.

In the midst of the chaos, sparked out between two broken chairs, is the man who shattered the aquarium.

Time to act, Danny thinks. He crouches over the body, feeling his pockets, making the quick moves he used to watch Jimmy Torrini do in the pickpocket routine. Long fingers working quickly. Easier when your mark is unconscious, of course.

A lighter, some cigarettes. A return ticket stub for the Star Ferry. Today's date. A receipt for a shoe repair outfit called Heart and Sole in somewhere called Wuchung Mansions. Danny commits them to memory and tucks them back in Pony Tail's pocket. He glances at the man's feet. One of his slip-on shoes has come loose and his foot is bare.

On the hard sole of his left foot is a neat tattoo – and there's the same pattern again! Forty-nine dots, seven by seven. Alongside are two Chinese characters.

黑龍

Again, one of the dots is circled – second column in from the right about halfway down. Is it the same as the one in the diagram at school? It's hard to remember and he curses himself for a moment for not 'paying attention to detail'. Dad would have grumped about that. Zamora comes over, shaking his head as he too clocks the pattern.

'Major,' Danny says. 'As your lifelong friend, tell me about this sign.'

'We'll talk later, Danny. Police will be here in a moment. That's the priority. Ah, there's my hat.'

He stoops to pick up his bowler and frowns. A hole had been blown through the crown. Zamora puts his index finger through it, waggles it thoughtfully, before reaching up to feel his head.

'Must have missed by millimetres!'

But Danny isn't listening. 'Can you at least remember if one of those dots on our hotel door was circled?'

'Does it matter?' Zamora snaps, his usual good humour now decidedly off balance. He stops himself short, holding his hands up in apology. 'Sorry, Mister Danny. Bad day.'

Danny nods. He still has the lighter in his hand. It's stamped in red with the same characters as on the man's foot – and quickly he shoves it into his jeans pocket.

But his thoughts have slipped to Sing Sing again, the sense of disappointment deepening. After all, her disappearance during the kidnapping is pretty suspicious. He thinks about the toughened hands, her defensive manner. He sees the challenging, direct smile sparking her eyes – and wonders what she meant about Dad. Where is she now? Back with her Triad friends? She must be with the bad guys – otherwise surely she, or Chow – would have stayed to help. Waited for the police. Maybe her interest was feigned and nothing more.

Zamora goes over to the pony-tailed thug and gives him a nudge with his boot. The man groans and rolls away. There, tucked under his thigh, is a little snub-nosed pistol. The Major looks around quickly, sees Danny is staring out into the street again, and then stoops to pick it up in one neat movement.

Over the sound of the rain on the restaurant's canopy comes the wail of a siren.

9 HOW TO READ SOMETHING HIDDEN FROM VIEW

The first police to arrive on the scene seem almost uninterested. When Danny and Zamora do eventually get to explain what has happened, the policemen simply shrug and seem more concerned with the damage to the restaurant.

'We need to get a damn move on,' Zamora barks. '*Comprende?*'

'Wait for boss,' the shorter one says. For a moment Danny is worried that Zamora will thump him, but the dwarf turns away abruptly, shoves his hands in his pockets and goes to stare out at the street.

The rain thickens, falling in curtains of water from the Bat's awning. Danny sits on a bar stool, thinking hard about the events of the last twenty-four hours. First, there was Laura's heightened alertness – as if she was expecting something. Then, Sing Sing mentioning Dad from out of nowhere. There was that unusual jagged edge to Zamora – even before the kidnap. And then there's White Suit and the stupid dots that keep turning up everywhere. But as to how these pieces fit together, he has no idea.

Ten minutes later a plainclothes policeman arrives, shaking the rain from his shaggy mop of hair.

'Senior Inspector Lo, B Division,' he says. 'Organized Crime and Triad Bureau.'

'We need to get a move on!' Zamora says, exasperated.

'Just need to go through details.'

Lo has sharp features, an intelligent face. A thin, white scar jags down his cheek. As he asks his questions he keeps glancing at Danny.

'I see. And tell me again *exactly* what your aunt was doing here?' he says, looking at Danny, interrupting Zamora's blow-by-blow description of the fight.

'She was investigating something called the Black Dragon—' Danny stops himself. Lo seems decent, but Laura's warning about corrupt police flips back into his head. Better to be on the safe side.

Lo pulls a face. 'Black Dragon?'

'Maybe it was something else,' Danny says quickly.

'Why don't we do this down at OCTB headquarters,' Lo says, motioning them towards his unmarked car outside. '*Much* quieter there. No prying eyes.'

'At least they got those two *idiotas*,' Zamora says, looking back up the street as they make their way through the puddles. Pony Tail is being led to a squad car, head bandaged heavily, eyes vacant, whilst the other man, still unconscious, is stretchered away to an ambulance.

And all this time, Danny thinks, the gang is spiriting Aunt Laura into the Hong Kong night. We should be out there. Doing something.

He frowns and then strides towards Lo's car.

They sit in the detective's cluttered office and wait.

And wait.

Three hours pass and the clock hands shudder slowly to half past midnight. People come and go in the corridor. Men in shirtsleeves, others in jackets stamped with OCTB in big yellow letters. Now and then somebody peers in, raises their eyebrows – and then drifts away again. Zamora drums his fingertips on the desk and the rain keeps tapping away on the skylight overhead.

Adrenalin and jet lag are tugging Danny in different directions. Hard to tell whether he's buzzing, or going under from the sleep deprivation. He shakes his head

– I must concentrate. Keep focused.

'Where's that *blasted* detective got to?' Zamora says, slapping the desk hard.

Danny looks out into the corridor, and, as he does so, the door opposite opens. Slumped in a chair, and brightly lit by a desklamp . . . is White Suit.

The drowsiness rips from Danny's system. Wide awake again. I knew it. I knew he was after us! So they've got him. Maybe now we'll get to the bottom of it. Maybe Laura won't take long to find. Maybe even by morning we'll all be sitting round the breakfast table laughing about the whole thing.

But then the man glances up, eyes widening a fraction as his gaze meets Danny's. It's hard to read the look. Could be surprise? Or anxiety? A bit of both. But there's also something conspiratorial in the look. Something that makes Danny wonder whether he's reading the situation correctly. White Suit gives a very small shake of the head – then someone kicks the door shut and the slam echoes down the corridor like a gunshot.

'Major—'

But at that moment Inspector Lo comes back. A smile on his face and two Styrofoam cups of coffee in his hands.

'Sorry to have kept you.'

'*Madre mia*. At last,' Zamora huffs.

'Thought you might need refreshment.'

Danny is about to ask about the man in the white suit – but then sees that little shake of the head again in his mind. Maybe not. With that movement the man was saying, 'don't say you've seen me.' Or 'keep quiet'. Something like that. Only an instinct, but there's not much else to go on right now.

'What we *need* is for you to get a move on,' Zamora says, jabbing the table.

Lo spreads his hands to placate. 'We have Miss White's description out to all units, all informants. Ports and border control. We'll hear something soon.'

'Will the kidnappers ask for a ransom?' Danny asks.

'Very likely. Your embassy has been informed.'

Lo lights a cigarette, looking down at the paperwork on his desk.

'What about the scumbags you caught at the Bat?' Zamora says.

'It seems they may not have been involved in the kidnapping, Mister . . . Zamora.'

'Of course they were!' the dwarf says, getting to his feet. 'We SAW it! And it's *Major* Zamora!'

'Please sit down,' Lo says, very calmly. 'It's a bit

more complicated. They claim *you* assaulted *them*, you see. They may press charges. One of them is badly concussed. And there's lot of damage in the restaurant.'

'But there were witnesses,' Zamora splutters.

'It seems nobody saw it happen.'

'One of them had a gun,' Danny says, frustration building. Maybe he can try something, attempt the mirror force again. Worth a try. Probably a tougher nut to crack though.

'But we find no gun,' Lo says, tapping the desk emphatically. Danny does the same and shifts his breathing to match the rise and fall of the detective's chest. He emphasizes it with a slight movement of his hand, fingers wafting up as Lo breathes in, down as he breathes out. In, out.

'What about Detective Tan? The one Miss Laura was trying to find?' Zamora presses.

'Detective Tan is on holiday, I'm afraid.'

'But Laura said—' Danny stops himself short in time. Need to focus.

'Hawaii, I believe.'

Lightning flashes in the skylight overhead. As Lo glances up at it, Danny does so too.

'What about the tattoo on the man's foot?' he says, trying to pace his voice into the hypnotic rhythm, the one Dad always used to relax, persuade, mesmerize his 'marks'. He opens his eyes wide, showing the colours. 'The pattern. You're going to tell me what those forty-nine dots are, aren't you!?'

The detective returns Danny's look, stubbing out his cigarette irritably. 'No idea,' he says. 'No idea at all. And the way we do things is that I ask questions. OK? You've had a shock. Let *me* do the police work . . .'

Danny sits back, deflated and rather embarrassed.

'And what about the Chinese characters next to it?' Zamora insists.

Lo fires up his laptop. 'They just say Kowloon, Mister Zamora. Nothing else. Now, just need to do one more form. P28. Shouldn't take twenty minutes. Maybe a little bit more.'

Danny groans. 'But if it was the Black Dragon, why can't you just go after them?'

'But we don't know it, do we?' Lo answers. 'And no one knows where they are.'

Disappointed with his attempt at the hypnosis, Danny idly watches the detective's fingers stump across the keys as Zamora spells out his name, profession – Circus Daredevil – Laura's details, their hotel name, what they did this last twenty-four hours.

It's interesting, he realizes; if you keep the image of

the QWERTY keyboard in your head you can tally
letters one by one to the keystrokes.

Z, A, M, O, R, A

G, O, L, D, E, N, B, A, T . . .

Intrigued, he sits up a bit and focuses as Lo punches
the keyboard two-fingered. Something's not quite
right, Danny realizes after a while. Not right at all. The
keystrokes aren't matching their answers. Not all the
time at any rate.

The phone rings.

'*Wai?*' Lo barks into the phone, grabbing a pen. He
scribbles on a Post-it pad.

'*Neih dim chingfu a?*' He's pressing very hard,
Danny thinks, the knuckles of Lo's hand white as he
grips the biro. Stressed.

The detective underlines what he has written, then
rips the note off the pad.

'Gotta go,' he says, grabbing his jacket. 'Busy night.
You go back to hotel. We'll do everything we can.'

An idea leaps into Danny's mind. He stands and
makes as if to shake Lo's hand.

'Thank you for your help—'

But as Lo reaches for his grip, Danny moves his
hand quickly sideways. The unexpected movement
confuses Lo's attention, and Danny's left hand sweeps

across the Post-it pad, whipping the second sheet.

'Sorry.' He shakes Lo's hand now firmly, palming the note like a playing card, transferring it to his back pocket in one smooth movement right under the detective's nose. Feels good to be doing something. And he has done it for good reason.

He's convinced that Lo has been less than straight with them.

The detective leads them out into the corridor. 'I'll have a couple of officers take you back to the Pearl. Keep to hotel. Don't trust anyone you don't know. If the Black Dragon are involved then we will all need to be careful.'

He adjusts the gun in his shoulder holster. 'Understand?'

Danny glances at the door that slammed on White Suit. There are raised voices coming from inside now, but indistinct. There's a muffled thud, like a heavy weight falling to the floor. Another – and then a stifled cry of pain.

Lo glances at the door, seems to hesitate a fraction, and then turns on his heels, striding briskly away down the echoing corridor.

Danny nods at the door, drops his voice. 'The white suit man's in there.'

'*Caray!* Why didn't Lo say?'

'I think he's being interrogated.'

'Maybe there's more to this than meets the eye,' Zamora says.

'You've no idea who he is? White Suit?'

'Not a clue.'

A police car takes them back to the Pearl on rain-slicked streets. So many lights overhead that they fuse into a white smoke in the humid air. Danny gazes up at them. The feeling that has been growing these last few days – that began with the explosion and that washed over him in the rain outside the Bat – is loud in his head. Something's coming. Something I've been trying to avoid, but can't avoid any longer. And ever since the trip began it has felt like Mum and Dad are closer again somehow. Their personalities, their actions conjuring themselves back to life around him.

He turns to Zamora beside him on the back seat of the patrol car. The dwarf's profile is giving nothing away except grim determination – the kind that used to play on his face when they were facing a difficult crowd or pitching the big top in a high wind. In the glow of the neon signs overhead he looks older than Danny remembers. Tired.

'At Mum and Dad's funeral you said I could always trust you.'

The dwarf shifts on his seat.

'Well, of course you can, Mister Danny. Let's keep focused on the immediate problem . . .'

But the memory of the funeral is stirred now. Danny remembers how well Zamora supported him then. Danny had found himself alone, standing in the steadily falling snow, the entire company of the Mysterium gathered under the skeletal trees in the Berlin Kreuzberg Friedhof. Darko Blanco was saying how hard it had been for the gravediggers. Pneumatic drills were needed.

Danny had desperately tried not to think about what Mum and Dad looked like in those long silent caskets. The worst of it was this: when you were used to seeing them escape from confined spaces – despite being bound and shackled – you couldn't help but assume that any moment now the coffins' lids would spring open, and there they would be, smiling and taking their bows after another daring stunt. But the lids stayed resolutely shut. And remained so. Danny had thought about Houdini's escapes from the 'living burials'. It was one trick his father never wanted to emulate. (He had started working on it, but couldn't cope when the soil hit his face, choking him. Each time he sat up and shook his head violently – and then got out of the open grave.)

In the cemetery Zamora had come up and stood next to Danny, letting his quiet presence do the work. After a long while watching the snow fall the dwarf had said, 'You can always rely on me, Danny. Always.'

Danny believed it then. He needs to believe it now.

10 HOW TO REVEAL HIDDEN MESSAGES

Thirty minutes later they're sitting by the window in their hotel room. Across the South China Sea the last of the lightning is guttering away to nothing.

Danny looks at Zamora. 'So you were going to tell me about the dots.'

The dwarf looks thoughtfully at his hat as he twirls it in his stubby fingers.

'Please.'

'I don't know much. Honest. Your aunt always keeps things close to her chest, you know. Mother of God, it was three weeks before anyone even knew she was in *prison*!'

'You were Dad's closest friend,' Danny presses. 'He trusted you. I *need* to know.'

'Well. There's always been a rumour. A rumour about a criminal organization – a global organization – that pulls all the strings behind the big gangs and crime families. That's what Laura told me. She got interested in it some time ago. But she was sure it was just a myth. Like Bigfoot, or UFOs. She thinks some gangs use it to scare people . . . you know, what do they call it – a bogeyman.'

'Go on.'

'Laura wrote about it a year or so ago. And then she got a number of anonymous notes and emails via her editor. That same symbol on each one. She thinks it's just some crank trying to put the wind up her and make out it really exists.'

'That what exists?'

'It's called the "Forty Nine". Because there are meant to be forty-nine members from affiliated gangs around the world. A kind of supercrime syndicate. Always forty-nine. When one dies – or disappears – another takes his or her place. Sounds fantastical really, but now with the dots turning up all over the place, well . . .'

'And what has it got to do with the Black Dragon?'

'Laura didn't say. She just wanted to bring you along to . . . show you Hong Kong. What with school being shut and all.'

'And that's all you know?'

Zamora turns to look out of the window, but

Danny catches his reflection in the glass. Caution. His hands are tensing slightly, as if holding on to something.

'That's all I know about the stupid dots.'

Something definitely unsaid. Danny goes to challenge him, and then decides to let it pass. He will trust Zamora. People always said that Zamora had the word 'honest' running through him like a stick of rock says 'Brighton'. If he's not being a hundred per cent truthful he must have his reasons. So forget about it for now. Find the right way forward.

It was Dad's contention that any problem – almost any problem – could be solved if you just broke it into small enough parts. He would sit Danny down, with a mug of tea for each, at the big table in the trailer, then write a problem in capital letters at the top like 'HOW TO DO THE BURNING ROPE ESCAPE'.

'But it could equally well be how to mend a tap or how to make a cup of tea,' Dad said. 'The principle is the same. I call it my "Atomic strategy." The main thing is that your problem contains masses of other little ones hidden inside it. Maybe ten, maybe a hundred. You have to take it to pieces, so it becomes something like: "how to escape from a burning rope, whilst you're held fast in a straitjacket and you only have sixty seconds to get free." Then you can see how to break it down further, stage by stage . . .'

He started to draw radiating lines, write down new subheadings, expanding the problem across the sheet.

'. . . And so, old son, the burning rope part has at least nine elements including thickness of rope, the kind of fuel you put on it and so on . . . and then those can subdivide.'

And pretty soon his tea would be cold and the paper would be covered in writing and lines.

'But that looks impossible,' Danny said.

'No, it's not. It just looks bad. But now all the problems are little ones. Solvable. It's just a matter of working through it one by one. You write them in the order you need to solve them and then you just go at it one at a time, Danny. Lock by lock, so to speak!' And then he crumpled up the paper into a tight ball, tucked it down into his left fist, blew on it – and it was gone, vanished into the bright light from the window. 'But we don't want anyone getting their hands on trade secrets, do we now?!'

Danny grabs his notebook. He takes a pen and writes down 'HOW TO RESCUE AUNT LAURA.'

He looks at the problem and adds a new line. 'How to find Aunt Laura. How to release her.'

Zamora looks over his shoulder. 'We'll need clues.'

'We've already got some,' Danny says. 'The man in the Bat had a Star Ferry ticket marked today. Yesterday, I mean. The ticket had our room number on the back. He must have been stalking us. And he had a shoe repair receipt for somewhere called the Wuchung Mansions.'

'How do you know?'

'From the man with the pony tail. I checked his pockets.'

'Maybe you should have left that to the police?'

Danny shakes his head. He writes down a new line: 'WORK OUT WHO TO TRUST.'

'What do you mean?'

'When we were answering Lo's questions, he wasn't typing what we said. Not all the time. I could see where his fingers were going. He typed our names all right. But when you said "Golden Bat" he typed something that had at least three "p"s or "o"s in it. Top right on the keyboard. Like "Happy House" for example. Something like that.'

'*Madre mia* – you sure?'

'Sure. Same again when we told him what Laura was doing in Hong Kong. He didn't type "journalist". I think it was "shopping"!'

'That's the last thing your aunt would do.'

Danny draws two lines from the last question and puts 'Detective Lo' and 'Detective Tan' in little boxes.

'Better add Charlie Chow to that list. I don't trust him at all,' Zamora says, tapping the sheet. 'Not at all. Made himself scarce. That girl too.'

Danny's hand hesitates for a beat. And then reluctantly he adds Sing Sing to the list.

'We might have one more clue here,' he says, taking the blank Post-it note from his back pocket. He holds the paper up to the light, turns it side on.

'I don't see what that's going to tell you,' Zamora says. 'I saw you swipe it, of course. Nicely done.'

Danny takes a 2B pencil from his bag and the craft knife he uses to sharpen it. He snaps the pencil in two, and quickly pares away the wood from one side, exposing the graphite core. He spreads the note out, rubbing the cored pencil across it.

'Clever lad!' Zamora says, leaning over.

Clearly revealed – negative white lettering through the graphite – is the imprint of what Inspector Lo scrawled on the sheet above.

A short string of Chinese characters – and two numbers below: a 4 and a 9. The goosebumps prickle up Danny's skin.

'Are you still sure this is just a wind-up, Major?'

'I'm not sure about anything to tell you the truth.'

'And Detective Lo claimed to know nothing about it. We need to find Laura's notebook. That's what she shouted as they pushed her into the car. It's the one she always keeps on her.'

He adds 'WHERE IS THE RED NOTEBOOK?' to the list of problems.

'Let's start at the Golden Bat. There must be a reason that Lo wanted to divert attention away from it.'

'I take it we won't be following his advice then?' Zamora says with a smile.

Danny shakes his head.

'But we're going to take my advice,' the dwarf says, straightening himself to his full height and stretching. 'We're going to eat something. And get forty winks. Recharge. No good running around on empty. We'd just make stupid mistakes. Like that time I fell off the Wall of Death. I was just tired.'

He rubs his thigh thoughtfully at the memory, the old break aching there like it always does when the weather's stormy.

'Strength and balance, Danny, that's what Rosa always said. Doesn't matter whether we're doing trapeze or acrobatics or voltige or cyr wheel or tightwire or cloud swing or any of the other skills. We always need to be balanced – and we always need to keep our strength up. That way we don't make mistakes. Take our ringmistress's advice even if you won't take mine.'

Danny nods, remembering the way Rosa could manage the wilder elements of the company. Get the best from everyone with her Italian charm. Or turn on the anger just when it was needed.

'You're right. But just a few hours. And then let's get on with it.'

11 HOW TO CONCENTRATE COMPLETELY

But sleep doesn't come easily for Danny.

He lies awake for an hour, then two – listening to sirens, the sounds of boats in the bay, while his mind churns images, thoughts, fears.

When he does drop off, it's into that strange halfway place again, into the borderland between waking and sleeping – his head blurred by the long-haul flight, sleep deprivation and shock. The last thing he's thinking about is the aquarium in the Golden Bat, and its tumbling bubbling water, the breaking glass, the fish.

The surge of water from the shattered tank repeats and his mind links one event to another, and slips a gear – and he's back there again, under the hemisphere of the Mysterium, standing beside the water torture cell.

His father has loosened the chains and is wrenching

himself up towards the top of the tank, working the ankle locks. His expression is slightly different from normal. But then, he has only ever done this in practice, never as a performance. He looks surprised. And rather tired. As if all the energy is draining out of him.

'Two minutes ten . . . fifteen,' Danny calls, his voice sounding small against the music. You can sense the expectant crowd, waiting, holding one long collective breath . . . Two minutes thirty is the limit and they're past it now. Come on . . .

His father makes one more assault on the ankle locks and suddenly flops back down. Defeated! A few more bubbles escape from the corner of his mouth, his gaze searching out Zamora's. A single shake of the head, eyes wide, imploring help. He is defeated.

And then it all goes very quickly. Major Zamora takes a mighty heave with the axe. *Clung.* It bounces back off the glass. The dwarf takes another swing and this time the glass splinters with a resounding crash. There is water everywhere. Simultaneously Danny can hear his father gasping for breath, retching, the crowd noise rising in uproar. Rosa Vega, their beautiful ringmistress, is stalling, her voice bright but faltering on the PA system.

The Khaos Klowns are coming on instead – they're

only half changed but are snapping into their emergency *charivari* act like they know to do when there's an accident or hiccup in the running order. They rush past, some of them in the skull masks, brandishing torches and fire staffs, some made up with the leering smiles that haunt Danny's nightmares. Roustabouts are rushing to pull Dad from the wreckage.

Darko Blanco is crouched over him, helping him to his feet, supporting his sagging weight. And Mum's there too, hurrying to Dad's side, eyes flashing in fear.

In the Pearl Hotel bedroom Danny's eyes pop open, as he snaps back out of the memory. He sits bolt upright, and knows that this time *something* had been added to the memory. Something he hasn't seen before. What is it? He grabs for the thought – but too hard. Like trying to hold on to a wet fish, it slips his grasp. And then the reality of where they are now, of what has just happened to Laura, comes rushing back and the dream memory is swamped.

Even a week ago he would have pushed the unwanted surge of memory to the back of his mind, but now he actively follows it. I need to start to remember properly, he thinks. Systematically.

So what can I remember if I choose? If I don't just

wait for the memories to come?

That night after the failed escape it was Blanco who helped Dad back to the trailer. We followed them and Mum told me not to worry. But I could see she was beside herself . . .

The knifethrower saw to it that Dad was comfortable, and turned to leave.

I never felt entirely at ease around Blanco, he thinks, but there was something cool about the way he did his meditation every morning. Back straight, eyes half closed, radiating calm. You felt he had a clarity in his pale-blue eyes. I stopped him on the trailer steps.

'Why did it happen, Blanco?'

'Why does *anything* happen?'

'Dad never makes mistakes.'

'But we all do. It's about concentration. Mindfulness. Can you count slowly to ten without thinking *one* thought? Without clutching at a single thought?' Blanco said. 'That's what we have to do when we try and escape from underwater. Or throw knives. Or push long nails through our noses . . . Concentrate one hundred per cent and think of nothing else.'

He smiled then. A sad smile.

'Maybe your dad just has a bit too much on his mind.'

* * *

It's Zamora who wakes him, shaking Danny gently by the shoulder, bringing him back from the sleep that has finally pulled him under.

'Rise and shine, Danny. Six in the morning.'

Danny rubs his eyes, sitting up, trying to get his bearings. 'Have they found her? Any news?'

'No. *Nada*. Nothing from kidnappers, or police. But you know what they say. No news is good news.'

It just doesn't feel like that though. Surprising that nobody has come to find them.

'Let's start working on our list.'

'Better than twiddling our thumbs, *no*?'

Zamora rummages in his trouser pocket and produces a card. 'And I was thinking maybe Kwan can tell us something about what your aunt got up to yesterday. Got his number here. I'll call him from the lobby. But first you're going to eat some breakfast.'

In the Pearl's foyer, a plasma screen is looping BBC World News, sound muted. The tail end of the ticker feed catches Danny's attention – and he keeps watching, waiting for whatever it was to come round again. The Prime Minister smiles and delivers a speech on the steps of No. 10. Then a famous footballer deadpans platitudes in a post-match interview. And then a still image of the rusting hulk of a cargo ship fills the screen – an ugly, squat vessel, with the headline MISSING CHINESE FREIGHTER.

The image shifts to shaky handheld footage of a kind of rubbish dump, protected by high fences that are dotted with yellow radiation signs. PIRATE HIJACK SUSPECTED: AUTHORITIES DENY LINK TO RADIOACTIVE CARGO, the caption reads, before the bulletin flips to the start and there's the newsreader and the PM opening his mouth again, stuck in the loop.

'*Vamos!*' Zamora says. 'I got hold of a dispatcher at Kwan's office. They'll get him to meet us at the Golden Bat.'

The heat's already building as they retrace their steps to Mong Kok. The streets are emptier and, in the clear light of day, the exoticism of last night is replaced by something harder. Crumbling concrete on some of the buildings. Peeling paintwork. Washing hanging out to dry in the gritty air while restaurant and shop owners scrub down the pavements.

They have expected to find police tape cordoning off the restaurant – or even an officer on duty – but there's nothing at all to suggest the events of the previous evening. The door and main window are blinded by graffiti-covered shutters, both padlocked tight shut. One small window is uncovered, gazing at the street blankly from just above them.

'You take a look, Danny. You've got the advantage over me now,' Zamora says.

Standing on tiptoes, squinting into the gloom, Danny can just make out the wreckage of the aquarium, shoved back against a far wall. Chairs are stacked on tables, but otherwise all the glass, broken furniture, water and dead fish have been cleared away.

'Can't see much.'

'We need to get inside,' Zamora grunts, rattling the shutter.

Danny touches the lock pick set on the end of its bootlace. Maybe it's the kind of simple padlock that springs easily?

He remembers Dad giving him the basic lessons and going on and on about Houdini's great moment of discovery as a boy when, working in an ironmonger's, he had been asked to free a convict from handcuffs. He had succeeded and – hey presto – that was the start of a whole career. Everyone has to start sometime, Danny thinks. Saw rake is the best bet when you're in a hurry. He flips open the pick set. Then cranks the lock with the tension tool and starts dragging the rake in and out, feeling the pins moving, trying to make them fall into the shear line. Nearly. Try again.

But then he hears footsteps approaching quickly and, guiltily, he snaps the tool shut.

Looking up he sees Sing Sing.

She's coming at a half trot down the hill, eyes hidden behind a big pair of wrap-around shades, a small rucksack slung over one shoulder. The sun catches her bright-green trainers. Danny feels something lift, as if a small weight has come off his shoulders. In broad daylight she looks like any other early teen – hardly like an enemy. He's glad to see her.

'What do we think about her?' Zamora whispers.

'Not sure,' Danny says. 'But it felt like she was waiting for something to happen last night—'

'Oi, *senorita*!' Zamora booms. 'We want a word—'

'What happened to you last night?' Danny says, cutting across the dwarf.

She comes close up to them, but then walks right on by. Zamora goes to grab her elbow but she sidesteps neatly and hisses, 'Shut up, dumdums. Follow me.' And hurries on.

'Nothing to lose,' Danny says. 'But let's keep our eyes peeled.'

Three shops further down the lane, Sing Sing swings round a corner into an alleyway. Danny tries to relax, open his senses up, eyes wide, scanning for trouble as they follow close behind.

The girl is moving at speed, ten or so paces in front of them, turning right again, into a much darker, narrower passageway that cuts along the back of the shops. She comes to a halt.

'Back door to Bat,' she says over her shoulder. 'I have a key—'

'Why did you disappear?' Danny interrupts. 'Where's Laura?'

Sing Sing shakes her head. 'No time. Not good to be seen around here. You want to look for something, right? Something that belongs to your aunt?'

'How do you know?'

'Lucky guess.'

'Now, listen, miss,' Zamora says. 'Where's Chow?'

With her eyes shrouded by the sunglasses it's very difficult to read anything on her face. 'No idea.'

Sing Sing looks away, her mouth set in a firm line. 'You coming or not, boys?'

Zamora glances at Danny. 'What do you think?'

'We'll take a look. But we need to ask you some things—'

'You got five minute,' Sing Sing says, shoving the key in the lock. 'Or we going to be in big flipping trouble.'

The metal door squeals open to reveal the Golden Bat kitchens.

A battery of pans and woks hang ready for the new day's work, the air fat with stale oil and soy. Cleavers racked on the wall. The image of the thugs waving those things at Laura is still fresh in Danny's mind – and a wave of nausea rises as he thinks of them hacking away at his aunt's fingers. He swallows hard.

'What you looking for?' Sing Sing says, flicking on the lights. Again that direct, abrasive tone. But it feels like there's something softer underneath, Danny thinks.

'Our business,' Zamora says. 'Are you in with these Triad boys?'

'Things *far* more complicated than that,' she says, taking off her sunglasses. In the fluorescent light Danny sees a fat bruise blooming under her right eye. On her clear skin, the thing looks ugly, out of place.

'You OK?' he asks, pointing at it. Must be hurting like anything.

'My own fault,' she snaps. 'Not fast enough. Now get a move on. The Triads have eyes everywhere. The chef will be here soon and he's *very* angry about his fish.' She returns Danny's gaze, looking directly into his eyes, and smiles again – briefly. Hard to fake a smile like that, he thinks. The micro-muscles around the eyes doing a lot of the work. Then it's gone – as if wiped away – and she turns to push through into the restaurant proper. 'Let's go.'

They follow her into the cavernous interior of the Bat.

The noise and confusion of last night is replaced now by brooding shadows, pooling around the stacked chairs and tables. The curling dragons leer from out of the gloom, their faces transformed, ominous.

Danny heads for the raised platform. 'Come on, Major. Let's search around our table first.'

'I keep watch for you,' Sing Sing says, going to stand by the small window. 'But be quick. Haven't got all day.'

'You check under it, Danny,' Zamora says. 'I'll look around.'

Danny gets down on hands and knees. Here and there you can see damp patches that haven't dried yet. Despite the darkness under the table it's obvious there's nothing on the floor. Swept and wiped after last night's confusion the wooden boards are clean and bare. One tiny fish – bright crimson – lies forgotten, tucked next to a table leg, drowned in the air. Danny shoves it with his fingertip. It doesn't move – just lies there looking surprised, mouth open, eyes glassy. Nothing else to be seen.

Disheartened, he scrambles back from under the table.

'Nothing?' Zamora asks.

Danny shakes his head and goes over to where Sing Sing stands by the little window, head silhouetted against the morning.

'What did my aunt do after you met her last night?'

'Not much. Usual kind of thing. Talked about you! Very interesting . . .' Again that knowing hint of a smile, slightly superior.

'Nothing else?'

Sing Sing wraps her arms round herself and shakes her head. There's something lonely about that action, he thinks. Closed in. It reminds him of the way he himself stands in goal at Ballstone when the game is raging down the other end of the pitch. Something protective, keeping yourself to yourself. Because you've been hurt and don't want to be hurt again?

Possibly. But no – it's something more immediate. Not a memory. There's something about the way Sing Sing is shielding her rucksack, as if guarding something valuable inside?

The girl laughs abruptly. 'What you staring at?'

'Nothing. I—' Danny shifts to one side, moving closer to the rucksack. Sure enough Sing Sing turns very slightly to hide it again.

'Are you trying to hypnotize *me*?!'

'I'm just thinking about a little red notebook of Laura's.' And yes, there it is. A tiny flicker of recognition on her face, registering the hit. 'I just wondered if you could hand it over now!'

Sing Sing smiles. 'Ve-ry impressive!'

She reaches into the rucksack and pulls out the elastic-bound notebook. It glows red in the narrow shaft of light from the window. 'Not bad, Mister Woo.'

'Why didn't you tell us straight away?'

'You didn't ask. And I wanted to see how clever you are!'

That softens his irritation. Her spiky exterior is working as a coping strategy, he realizes. Give her the benefit of the doubt.

He looks down at the notebook and starts to riffle the pages, hiding his embarrassment at the compliment.

Zamora has seen the exchange and hustles over to peer at the book.

Together they scan Laura's jumpy handwriting to find the last few entries.

Under yesterday's date they see: *12.30. No sign Tan. 'Sick leave'. No reply phone.*

Another: *Meet Chow Golden Bat 7.30pm. Well St.*

The last, underlined and in capitals: *B DRAG – W. M.?*

'B DRAG must be Black Dragon,' Zamora says. 'But what about W. M.? Who's that?'

'Don't know,' Danny says. 'White Man? Like White Suit?' He looks at Sing Sing. 'Do you know who W.M. could be?'

'Sorry.'

A car rumbles past outside, belting out Chinese pop. It's closely followed by the waspy buzz of a scooter. The engine slows and idles outside for a second or two, before dragging away down the street. Sing Sing turns to peer out of the window.

'We gotta go. Triad boy, I think.' She spins and goes flying back across the restaurant, her feet whispering on the floor. 'See you around!'

'But—' Danny begins.

'Good luck,' she shouts, weaving round the tables.

Her slim form perfectly in balance, a spring and poise in each step.

'Come on, Danny,' Zamora says. 'Follow her!'

But by the time they are through the kitchens the back door is already banged shut.

And as they run out into the service lane, Sing Sing has vanished. Just a vague sound of footsteps echoing off the walls. Hard to tell whether they come from left or right – or, by a trick of the ears, from somewhere overhead.

Zamora puffs out his cheeks. 'Best make ourselves scarce. Something must have spooked old Sing Sing, *no*? Mister Kwan should be here soon.'

'We shouldn't have let her go.'

Danny strains to listen for the retreating footsteps. They've gone now. There's frustration at the way Sing Sing has toyed with them – she must have known we were after the notebook all along, he thinks. But there's another feeling mixed with it: disappointment that they've lost her again.

There's no sign of the scooter when they peer out into the street.

But Kwan is already waiting, further down, tucked deep in the early morning shadows at a safe distance.

He flashes his headlights once, then leans out to beckon them over.

'Come on, come on,' he says as they reach the battered car. 'Get in quick. I don't want people to see me round here. Triad lookout just went past.' His owlish face looks really nervous this time, as if his glasses will steam up.

Danny and Zamora nip onto the back seat, and Kwan's pulling away hard before they've even got the door shut, up the street, past the Golden Bat. The driver glances in his rear-view mirror, mashing the gears.

'Just in time,' he says as they turn right at a crossroads and merge into a traffic jam. 'We all in trouble if we seen there. Believe me.'

12 HOW TO FIND A DRAGON'S LAIR

But he seems to relax a bit as they put distance between themselves and the restaurant.

'So sorry to hear about Miss White. I'll do whatever I can to help.'

'We need to check somewhere out, Mister Kwan,' Zamora says. 'What was the name of those Mansions, Danny?'

'Wuchung.'

'Do you know where that is?'

Kwan recoils, as if catching a nasty smell at the back of the throat. 'That's bad place. Not nice. Old apartment block. Cheap hostels, drugs, bed bugs, bad people. You don't want go there . . . Even cops go in threes. Armed.'

'Just like where I grew up,' Zamora says grimly. 'Sounds great.'

'We're going there, Mister Kwan. We have to.'

Kwan sucks his teeth. 'OK. I take you. But I drop you short, and you don't tell *anyone* I take you there. Not *anyone*. OK?'

'OK,' Danny says. 'But can you tell us where you took my aunt yesterday?'

The traffic has ground to a halt again and Kwan turns round. 'All over place. Happy Valley, the racecourse, Mong Kok. The Peak. She was looking for someone all afternoon. We went to lots of places and I waited. She got bit angry. Really annoyed about something. Not me. Then she ask me to go to Golden Bat. I drop her there seven forty-five. Go home. Wife was very cross.' He sighs.

They're moving again. There's a scooter whining close up their exhaust and Kwan throws it a quick look in the mirror.

Danny takes a chance. 'Do you know anything about something called the Black Dragon?'

A flicker of recognition in the driver's eyes.

'Maybe I read about them in the paper. Triad guys.' He pulls a face. 'Low life.'

'And what about something called the Forty Nine?'

This time Kwan's face is as blank as a sheet of paper. 'No idea. Forty-nine what?'

'We think they're involved with the kidnap,' Danny says.

'What do police say?'

'They're looking into it,' Zamora says heavily.

They thump across a junction and into a canyon of a street, the buildings crowding overhead.

Danny sits back and flicks the pages of Laura's notebook. The last five or six seem to contain notes for the investigation, but it's hard to decipher her scrawl. He can just make out the odd word or two. *CARGO, PIRACY? WANSHAN ISLANDS.* Tucked between pages is a folded newspaper clipping and he opens it up to reveal a photo of Chow, standing impassively on the harbour front. Same stony expression on his face. The headline says: BUSINESSMAN DEFIES THE NEW DRAGON.

Danny shows it to Zamora.

'But look what's below in the subheading,' the dwarf says.

'*Former gang boss says he has turned new leaf in fight for law and order in Hong Kong—*' Danny reads aloud.

'They all say that,' Kwan snorts. 'But they're all on the make.' He brings the taxi to a swerving stop by the pavement. 'Mansions just down there.'

He points at the ugly mass of a building across the

road. Its first two storeys are covered in garish advertising for everything from currency exchange to massage to karaoke. Above that it rises some twenty or more floors, grey and heavy, sprouting air-conditioning units like carbuncles, the roof bristling with aerials and weeds. It does not look at all savoury – or inviting. A constant stream of people is being swallowed or spat out of its gaping mouth.

'Looks like a fortress,' Danny says uncertainly.

'You should have seen old Hong Kong, sir. Kowloon Walled City. Much worse.' Nostalgia softens Kwan's face. 'A *gweilo* like you wouldn't have gone in there.'

'*Gweilo?*'

'Pale ghost. Foreigner.'

Danny feels deflated at that. He glances in the rear-view mirror. It's true, he realizes. Here in Hong Kong he looks decidedly Caucasian against the people thronging the streets all around. But at Ballstone he always felt conscious of Mum's Chinese genes shining through in his black hair, the shallow curve of his eyes. Before the fire, safe in the cosmopolitan bubble of the Mysterium, he never thought much about nationality or race. It always seemed incidental to what people did. What they said. Since then though, that need for 'fit' has been nagging away steadily.

He sighs, feels in his pocket for money for the fare and pulls out the Post-it note instead. He leans forward to show it to Kwan.

'Can you read this for us?'

The taxi driver squints at the characters.

'Terrible writing. It says "Sai Wan Pier, Cheung Chau Island".'

'*M goi.*' Danny says experimentally, rolling the Cantonese around his mouth. Thank you. It feels like he's tasting a food he hasn't tried for years and years. Kwan nods in answer.

'Don't mention it.'

'Could you take us there later?'

'I can take you to the ferry,' the driver says, patting the steering wheel, 'but the roads on the island are too small for cars like mine. You take care in Mansions. Keep in busy areas. Call me if you need. I gotta get home to Mrs Kwan. *Baai baai.*'

Danny and Zamora jostle through the tourists and touts on the pavement outside the building. Above them the building rises like a rock face. Young men tug their sleeves, shouting out amazing deals to be had inside – or whisper more shady offers on the floors above.

'You want to get happy, gentlemen?'

'Best curry outside Bombay.'

'You want fortune read? Guaranteed good fortune?'

Above the doors a sign reads: 'Wuchung Mansions. Luxury Accommodation Since 1952'.

'In a hurry,' Zamora mutters. 'Excuse us . . .'

But Danny stops dead in the flow of people, pointing up at the sign.

'W. M., Major. Wuchung Mansions. It's got to be this place. After all, we know Pony Tail has been here. And Black Dragon must be linked to it somehow.'

13 *HOW TO HYPNOTIZE A HOODLUM*

The ground floor is a sprawling labyrinth of tiny shops and restaurants. The bleating of electronic gadgets merges with the rattle of slot machines, the aroma of curry sauce muddled with the stink of laundry bleach.

Danny and Zamora wander deeper into its heart, blinking in the gloom, feeling like visitors from another planet.

People scuttle in the shadows. There are voices raised everywhere talking in a babble of Cantonese, Hindi, Thai, English, Japanese. Again the exotic surroundings bewitch Danny's senses – and yet, behind that, there's a familiar note to the sounds and smells. The basic greetings and sing-song politenesses of Cantonese coming vaguely back to him from his infancy. He himself may not look that Chinese, but he can imagine Mum gliding through a place like this. In her element. She would have done it with the same grace that guided her along the highwire every night. The stillpoint in the storm, oblivious to the punked-up antics of the Khaos Klowns as they filled the arena below with flame and smoke and the snarl of chainsaws.

In the glancing view of strangers who turn to look at them now he sees here a nose, there a cheek, there the same slim shoulders – and recognizes Mum piece by piece. The emotion rises, a tight knot of grief that wants to do its thing – but he knows he has to keep his head clear now.

Zamora tugs his arm.

'There it is, Danny: Heart and Sole.'

'Let me try something. You keep watch.'

Danny walks into the kiosk, trying to look confident – his heartbeat quickstepping all the same – and raps on the counter.

A man with a hangdog face looks up from the workbench, eyeing Danny with idle curiosity.

'*Jou sahn*. A friend of mine left shoes. He told me to pick them up.'

The man raises his eyebrows. 'Receipt?'

'He lost it. But he's got a long pony tail. Broken nose. About your height.'

The man frowns.

'You're a friend of Tony's!?'

'Yes,' Danny says firmly. 'Tony. He said be quick. Chop chop.'

The man frowns again, then turns to rummage through a stack of re-soled shoes. He finds the ones he's looking for and plops a pair of garish snakeskin slip-on shoes on the counter. There's a ticket attached to them.

The man looks at Danny and narrows his eyes now, as if not sure whether he's doing the right thing. He holds up his right hand. 'Five dollars. Five.'

He keeps one hand on the shoes, hesitating.

'You can ring him if you need,' Danny says, dropping a ten-dollar bill onto the counter. 'But he said to hurry. Keep the change.'

The man picks it up, considers, then slips the shoes quickly into a bag and waves him away like a bad smell.

Back outside, Danny pulls the shoes from the bag, and scans the counterfoil. But where there might have been a full name and address there's just one indecipherable character scrawled in biro along with the fee. Dejectedly he goes to join Zamora.

'We're close. But we've only got half a name. And we can't search the whole building. That would take days.'

'Let's watch from across the street,' Zamora says. 'Maybe something'll turn up.'

They drift back into the rush of the morning, their spirits sinking.

But sometimes it only takes a second for your luck to change. A quick shift in the shape of the world and there's an opportunity to be seized. If you're paying attention – if you don't hesitate – you can seize it.

As Danny and Zamora push back out onto the pavement, Pony Tail almost slips by them in the crowd. There's a bandage around his forehead and he's moving with a slight limp, but there's no mistaking the lean face, the hair.

Before he has time to think, Danny is pushing quickly towards the man. Zamora close behind, straining to see what Danny has seen – and when he does he bellows out, 'You! We want a word, Mister Hair!'

Pony Tail looks up, turns, and darts away through the muddle of touts and shoppers on the pavement. He has a good head start, and for a moment Danny thinks they will lose him in the chaos. But then Pony Tail trips over a suitcase and goes sprawling across the ground.

Danny's blocked by a group of confused backpackers, but the Major moves surprisingly fast and is quickly alongside the prostrate figure. For all the world it looks as if he's helping the man up.

'There you go, *amigo*. Easy now.'

But as Danny joins them, he's shocked see the little pistol snug in the dwarf's grip. He's showing just enough for Pony Tail to see, urging him to his feet, using his body to shield the gun from view.

'Get up slowly and then down this passageway,' Zamora hisses, shoving the man towards a narrow passage cut between the Mansions and the building next door. 'Not a peep, *comprende?*'

The man nods and allows himself to be guided down the alleyway. It's dark in there, choked with rubbish and the stench of urine. The buildings rise up like the sides of a well, a mess of pipes and hanging wires silhouetted against a slice of sky above.

'Not a word,' Zamora says again, gun hard against the man's back. 'You savvy?'

The man nods again, pony tail twitching, taken aback by the ferocity in Zamora's eyes. There's no doubting he means business.

'No problem.'

'That's right,' Zamora says. He shoves the man

further into the shadows, with Danny following, glancing back at the street to see if they have been spotted. No – the world goes on as if nothing untoward is happening.

'Now, tell us, my friend, nice and quickly, where is Miss White? Where is the lady you peabrains kidnapped yesterday?'

Pony Tail shakes his head. 'Not understand.'

'It's Wuchung Mansions, isn't it? *Isn't it?* But which floor? Which room?'

'No say.'

'*Ay caramba!* We haven't got time to mess about.'

The gangster looks genuinely scared, Danny realizes. Pupils massively dilated, muscles around them tightening. Jaw rigid.

'You've got three seconds,' Zamora says. '*Uno, dos . . .*'

'He won't say,' Danny whispers. 'He's more scared of them than us. Probably sworn an oath to the gang, death by a thousand cuts or something like that if he tells us. Much worse than you shooting him.'

He's thinking fast. How to make the most of this situation? Maybe this is the moment to put training into practice. After all, the mirror force on the stewardess went well – even if Lo didn't succumb to the technique. Perhaps I need to go for something quicker and more direct.

'I've got a better idea. Let's talk . . . much . . . more . . . calmly. Relaxed.'

Almost as if he can hear Dad whispering instructions: *That's it, Danny, keep the eye contact, drop your voice, use your hand to work their vision . . . keep using their name and you relax and they relax and you relax and . . .*

He takes the pick set from around his neck. It flashes in the shadowy alleyway, catching Pony Tail's attention. Danny locks his gaze with the gangster.

'Tony. I want you to listen very carefully. We can sort this out. Just have a look at this!' He holds the pick at eye level and then brings it rapidly towards the man's eyes, crowding his vision.

'Watch my hand, watch my hand. There you go.'

Pressing the cold steel to the man's forehead, he reaches round and holds the back of Tony's head with his other hand, pushing it forward and down, taking control.

'Sleep, Tony. *Wan an.*'

The Chinese words pop into his mouth. Mum used to say that every night when he was small: good night, sleep peacefully.

And the man does just that!

It's a perfect 'snap induction', textbook stuff. You've got the right subject up out of the crowd and they're looking around sheepishly – or grinning at a friend – and you get their attention, invade their space, confuse them, give them the command . . . and down they go. Out cold sometimes, if you're lucky.

And maybe it's helped by the fact that Zamora has knocked concussion into the man not twelve hours before; maybe it's the fear in the man's mind. Conflicting interests . . . who knows? Maybe it's just beginner's luck, like the young Houdini fiddling the lock of the cuffs and surprising himself as much as the convict as they sprang open, and a legend was born . . . As soon as Danny touches the lockpick to the forehead, Pony Tail's under, eyes glazed, out for the count.

'You sleep now,' Danny says, very quietly, suppressing the mixture of elation and surprise surging through him. '*On min*. Eyes closed, Tony. Deeeper. Just listening to my voice. Breathing in and oooouuut.'

Pony Tail's breath is shifting into a slower gear. Head heavy in Danny's hands. He feels his confidence growing, his voice calming himself as much as the man.

Zamora is struggling to fight back a grin.

'OK,' Danny says. 'Eyes open, but still verrryyy relaxed. And then you can just start thinking about where Laura is. Where is she? No matter how hard you try you can't help thinking about the room, the building. There she is now in your mind. You try not to, but it's as clear as day.'

He nods to the Major, who now slips the gun into his jacket pocket. The barrel juts against the fabric, keeping Pony Tail covered, just in case.

'It's all fine, Major,' Danny says. 'We can relax. Like Tony here. He doesn't have to tell us anything.'

As long as Pony Tail doesn't think he's betraying the gang it should be possible to get him to reveal it by slight movements from his body, subconscious signals. Danny shakes his fingers loose and then places both hands lightly on the man's shoulders.

'Just keep thinking – really seeing in your mind – how you would go to find your friends . . . forward or back. Left or right. How would you start?'

And then, as if sleepwalking, the man twitches and Danny reads the impulse and guides Pony Tail back out of the alley, slow step by slow step, like a sleepwalker, towards the pavement.

'That's it,' Danny says. 'Just keep that picture in

your head . . . We'll go this way, shall we? Left, isn't it?'

Pony Tail's muscles move under Danny's fingers. Yes.

Zamora whistles under his breath. 'No way, Mister Danny. Hellstromism!'

Danny doesn't answer – he's focusing carefully, keeping the lightest touch he can on the man's shoulders, sensing every resistance, every slight change of body angle. Dad used to play it with him as a kind of game – and it used to be a big part of Harry's routine. But this is going better than any of those tries he had at muscle reading – hellstromism – at the Mysterium. Maybe Pony Tail's so jumpy that the movements are easy to read? Who cares. It's working.

They're out of the stinking alleyway and passing unnoticed in the hustle and bustle. Danny tries not to second-guess any movement of his mesmerized subject. But Pony Tail transmits each change of direction as clearly as if he's telling them which way to go.

They turn left, back in through the doorway of the Mansions. Back into the labyrinth, past the little shops on the ground floor, past Heart and Sole, past the bedlam of the lifts with their blinking security cameras, the mobile phone shops, the tailors . . . All the while Pony Tail's movements are talking to Danny's fingertips as if saying, 'Yes, this way, over here, no, not that way, to the back here.'

They come to a fire door at the back of the ground floor. Danny nods to Zamora, who darts forward, holding it open, and they edge through. The door springs shut behind them, and cuts the noise of the Mansions to a distant hum.

In this sudden silence there's just the sound of their footsteps on the bare concrete and Danny's voice reassuring Pony Tail. 'Just keep seeing it in your head. Up the stairs? OK.'

They climb two flights of stairs and find themselves in a grubby but empty corridor. A handwritten sign on a door says 'Deluxe Delightful Rooms'. It looks as far from deluxe as you could get. Pony Tail is moving more quickly now, urgency transmitting up through Danny's fingers, into his arms. They pass a takeaway curry place, pans bubbling on dodgy-looking gas burners, and, beyond that, a room crammed with women bent over chattering sewing machines. Then down a long, echoing service corridor back into silence.

Pony Tail's feet stutter and he comes to a stop in front of the door of an ancient lift. A sign taped to it: OUT ORDER.

'Try it anyway,' Danny says. 'He wants to use it, I'm sure.'

Zamora punches the call button and, somewhere far overhead, a grinding starts to shake the lift shaft. The Major wrinkles his moustache.

'Needs some oil, wouldn't you say? Is old ugly here still under?'

'Really deep.'

The lift door judders open. As they step in the whole thing swings perceptibly, and Zamora casts wary eyes at the floor.

Danny looks at the control panel. Twenty-four numbered buttons as well as G for ground floor and B for basement. The alarm button is plastered over with red insulation tape. Not very reassuring.

Careful not to break all contact with Pony Tail, Danny moves his fingertips to the back of the gangster's right hand.

'OK, just think about the floor number. The floor where you want to go. You don't have to move your arm, just say it over and over in your head.'

Pony Tail's hand jerks up like an automaton, his finger extending, hovering near the 17.

Zamora presses it and the lift jerks skywards. Grinding metallic sounds reverberate from overhead, as the compartment groans and bumps against its shaft. The Major starts to whistle softly under his breath, eyes glued to the display ticking up the numbers.

'*No hay problema, no hay problema,*' he mutters to himself.

'*No problema,*' Pony Tail parrots from deep in his hypnotic state.

And then the lift comes to a stop at 17. Zamora grips the pistol tighter.

The doors open to reveal a dingy corridor, its walls running with damp. Deathly silence and no air. From somewhere a long way off comes the sound of hysterical laughter. It stops abruptly as they step out of the lift.

'Madhouse,' Zamora says.

Danny steadies his own breathing again.

'Just keep that image strong,' he says to Pony Tail, but the man needs no encouragement. He's transmitting again. A sensation of rush, a determination to get to wherever they're going. Muscles tensing.

'Easy now,' Danny says. 'No rush. Relaxed.'

Past a string of unmarked doors, up half a flight of steps, down another mouldering corridor, through a kind of interior bridge to another block, through a door, another dark passageway . . .

'*Madre mia,*' Zamora mutters. 'Hope we can find

our way back out of this.'

Pony Tail is hesitating now. Maybe the fear of revealing the hideout is starting to override everything else. The sensation of movement is dying under Danny's fingertips. It feels like he wants to stop . . . here.

'OK,' Danny says. 'Nothing to worry about. Shall we go on?'

But the man has come to a resolute halt outside an opaque glass door.

A plaque on the outside: BLACK DRAGON KUNG FU CLUB. And two characters under the words Black Dragon:

黑龍

Danny raises his eyebrows. Same characters surely. He takes Pony Tail's lighter from his pocket, studies it for a second and hands it to Zamora. 'Don't think Lo translated things properly for us. Do you?'

The dwarf shakes his head. 'Scumbag.'

They listen hard at the door. Not a sound from inside.

'Laura's here?' Danny asks quietly.

And Tony nods, as if lost somewhere very, very far away.

14 HOW TO WRITE WITHOUT A PEN

Zamora tries the handle, but it's locked.

There's a security code pad on the doorframe, and Danny's just considering whether he can get Pony Tail to reveal the number when the dwarf takes matters into his own hands. He charges the door, his left shoulder crunching into it just above the lock. It gives slightly. Zamora furrows his brow, takes another run up and the door wrenches loose, the frame splintering. It swings on one hinge and then crashes to the floor in a cloud of dust.

The noise reverberates in the corridor like a bomb going off – and snaps Pony Tail from his trance. He opens his eyes, blinks rapidly as he takes in the situation, then he's off at speed, round the corner and gone.

'Forget him,' Danny says. 'Let's see what we've got here.'

They dash through an office and, beyond that, find

themselves in a large echoing gymnasium. A row of dusty windows spill opaque light onto the wooden floor. Arrayed along the opposite wall is an arsenal of clubs, sticks and barbells. In front of those a wooden army of dummy fighting figures stand ready for sparring, their stocky arms held up stiffly, while black and white photos of stern kung fu masters stare down at them from the walk.

'Laura?' Zamora calls.

A punchbag twists very slowly on its rope, groaning. Not a soul to be seen and the silence sings in their ears.

At the far end of the gym there are two frosted glass doors. And one of them is ajar.

Watched by the life-sized dummies, they move across the wooden floor, senses straining. Still not a sound to be heard. Weird when you think how loud the rest of the city has been, Danny thinks. He reaches the half-open door – listens hard – then shoves it with his foot.

Inside there are ten or so camp beds crammed together, covered with a tangle of sleeping bags, blankets and kit bags, unwashed rice bowls, cups, teapots, overflowing ashtrays. Smoke and sweat hangs heavy on the air.

'Smells like the Khaos Klowns trailer after a show,

no?' Zamora wrinkles his nose. 'Think they were too bad-assed to use deodorant or something.'

Danny picks up a half-emptied cup. The coffee is scummed over, but still lukewarm.

'Can't be long gone. Let's try the other room.'

The second door squeals appallingly on its dry hinges, loud against the silent gym beyond, making them pause and listen. But there's no answering sound.

This room is smaller, almost empty. It contains a single camp bed and – thrust in a corner – Laura's leather shoulder bag! Danny's heart thumps hard in his ears as he goes to pick it up.

'She must be close,' he says. 'She's here somewhere!'

'Or was here.'

Something crunches under Danny's foot and he looks down to see the guts of what looks like a laptop. Chips, keys, black casing hacked to bits. Laura's is black.

'She's going to be mad about that,' Zamora says.

'But where is she?' Danny moans. She must be here. It's gone so well, following the clues, reading Pony Tail, penetrating this labyrinth. There must be some reward! But apart from the bag, the wreckage of the laptop, there's nothing else to see. Three acupuncture charts in frames hang at uncertain angles on the grubby wall, their bodies pierced by hundreds of black dots.

'Miss Laura!' Zamora shouts suddenly. 'Miss Laura, can you hear us?'

His voice booms out into the gym beyond.

Any thrill Danny has felt about the success of the hellstromism is fading – replaced by a growing sense of failure. He bites his lip, thinking hard, the bag still in his hands. It feels lighter than normal and he peers in. Virtually empty, the usual jumble of reporter pads, cough sweets, pens all gone – along with her wallet. He shakes it upside down and a packet of hankies and a lipstick go rattling out across the floor. The top's missing from the stick and it leaves a red gash on the boards.

That's unusual. For one thing Laura seldom wears the stuff, and – if she does – she always takes special care of it. 'After all,' she would say, 'it's only once in a blue moon that I slap it on.' She'd have hardly paused to put on make-up in the midst of being kidnapped, would she?

Zamora has wandered back into the gym and is still bellowing, '*Laura! Laura!*' Not the best of ideas, Danny thinks. But you can't hold a strongman back forever. He looks at the lipstick mark on the floor and a thought strikes him. Quickly he unzips the bag wide, turns it inside out, but there's nothing to see. No messages. The packet of hankies still sealed. He glances around the room.

The acupuncture charts stare back at him. One of them shows a narrow slice of clean wall between its frame and the pervading grime. Must have been moved recently. Danny goes over and shoves it with his finger revealing more clean white wall underneath. A bit more . . .

And there's the message he's looking for.

CHEUNG CHAU, it says in chunky lipsticked writing.

And, under it, scribbled in haste, LOOK FOR WHITE SUIT BE CAREFUL.

He looks down again at the gouge of lipstick on the floorboards. For some reason it holds his attention and makes him think of the dead fish on the floor of the Bat. And that should link to something else, he thinks. Something important that I can't grasp. But what?

It'll have to wait. Right now we need to get to this Cheung Chau place.

From outside comes the sound of footsteps pounding the wooden floor of the gym, and Zamora's shouting at the top of his lungs: 'Mister Danny! *Gran problema!*'

15 HOW TO OVERCOME VERTIGO IN PEOPLE OF SHORT STATURE

The Major is waving his pistol to and fro, confronting a semicircle of thugs. They're a mix of builds and ages, but all look like they've come through a lot of bad living to find themselves in the Black Dragon – their eyes are hard, glittering, glaring intently at Zamora and Danny. Pony Tail's tucked amongst them, shaking his head as if clearing a bad dream.

'Keep back,' Zamora shouts, 'or I'll drop you where you stand.'

The men edge closer, not convinced.

'Mister Danny,' the dwarf whispers, 'this pop gun's not loaded. I took the bullets out – to be on the safe side. Make a run for that fire door. I'll hold them off.'

'But—'

'Stay back!' Zamora thunders, backing around the wall with Danny close beside. 'Unless you want bullet acupuncture!'

Suddenly he drops the gun, grabbing a huge barbell off the wall. He hurls himself at the gang members, spinning the barbell hard, his tattoos and muscles twitching, flexing.

Danny goes scrambling for the fire door, glancing back over his shoulder. Zamora has already knocked two Triads to the floor, and the others are momentarily taken aback by the force of his attack. One of them pulls a gun from his baggy trouser pocket, but Zamora spots it and brings one end of the barbell smacking down on the thug's hand. The man howls, wrist cranked at a horrible angle, and the gun clatters to the floor. Gang members peel off, grabbing sticks and cudgels from the walls.

Danny pushes at the fire door, but it won't budge. Glancing over his shoulder, he sees Zamora retreating slowly, blocking blow after blow, edging towards him. A wooden sword shatters against the barbell.

'*Vamos!*' Zamora grunts, shoving the barbell into a thug's stomach. The man collapses, all the wind driven from his lungs.

Danny takes a deep breath, and kicks the bar hard. It still doesn't budge. Refocus, Danny. Need to imagine the strength. Imagine energy building in your belly, legs like metal. Take a deep breath and then release down through the leg, the foot, through the door right to the other side. Now!

It bursts open, taking out a gang member lurking on the other side. His face is astonished, then blank, as he keels to the floor.

'Come on, Major!'

Zamora parries one more blow, then, with all his strength, hurls the barbell two-handed at his adversaries.

'Let's go!'

They're through the door and slamming it shut before the gang manages to close. 'Need to brace it,' the dwarf shouts, looking around frantically.

A fire extinguisher – rust spotted with age – is leaning against the wall. Zamora grabs it and jams it under the door's external handle, wedging it up and locked.

'It'll buy us a few minutes. Now what?'

'Find a way out.'

'What about your aunt?'

'They've taken her somewhere else. I'll explain later.'

The landing is dark now, choked with cardboard boxes that fill the space and overflow down the stairs. Each one stamped with Chinese characters. Zamora cranks the lighter into flame and peers at them, running his finger along the English underneath. WING LUCK FIREWORK COMPANY. EXPORT. FLAMMABLE.

Angry voices yell on the other side of the door. The first thump as the gangsters make an effort to break it open. The door gives slightly but the extinguisher holds fast.

'This way for the exit then,' the dwarf says, holding the lighter over his head.

They hurry down the darkened stairwell, but haven't got more than half a flight when they hear voices echoing below them. A second later comes a deafening gunshot, the bullet ripping out a chunk of wall just above Zamora's head, showering them both with plaster.

'*Caramba*, Mister Danny. These jossers mean business!'

'We'll have to climb instead.'

Going back past the gym door they can hear the effort to break it down: a steady *boom, boom* as the door is rammed with something heavy. The fire extinguisher shifts again, making an ominous drawn-out hissssss.

'Keep climbing, Major.'

But Zamora pauses, looking at the boxes. He bends to one at the bottom of a stack and holds the lighter's flame steadily against it. It catches, takes hold, sending bigger flames licking up the box's side – glinting on the dwarf's face. He smiles.

'Light at arm's length. Oh boy. Run, Danny! As fast as you can. Don't wait for me!'

Danny climbs swiftly, but pauses at each landing to wait for Zamora. The voices below are climbing faster for sure, closing the gap. There's not much time.

'Come on, Major!'

'It's all right for you, Mister Danny. This is where my build holds me back, you know.'

Smoke is curling up the stairwell, stiffening the air. As Danny arrives at each new landing, he tries the door, but every single one of them is locked tight shut.

'This place is a deathtrap, Mister Danny,' the Major says, puffing hard, as yet another refuses to budge. 'Somebody ought to close the whole thing down.'

From below comes another gunshot, then another. They're deafening in the confined space and a bullet ricochets off the metal handrail setting it ringing.

Then a moment later there's an eruption of sound below – something like machine gun fire; loud, stuttering. The corridor is lit up by flash after flash as the box of firecrackers ignites and detonates. And that sets off a chain reaction: rockets scream and bang in the gloom, Roman candles pump out their flares, brilliant and extraordinarily loud in the echo chamber of the stairwell. Bursts of blue, green, luminous orange. A rocket comes hurtling up out of the chaos and goes fizzing crazily off the walls and the smoke billows blackly towards them.

And then, amidst the chaos, a deeper explosion that rocks the stairs.

'Fire extinguisher, *no*?' Zamora says, rather proudly.

'Good job,' Danny says, patting him on the back. 'Even better than the end of the *Wonder Chamber*.'

They come to the top floor. No more steps, and the stairwell below engulfed in smoke as the fireworks display stutters to a close. A number on the wall says 24. No doorway here, just blank wall. Above them a trapdoor is cut into the ceiling with an extendable ladder clamped tight against it. EMERGENCY ROOF ACCESS, a sign says, but the steps are well out of both Danny's and Zamora's reach. The smoke is stinging their eyes, making them gag.

'There ought to be laws,' Zamora says. 'What about equal opportunities? I'll bunk you up.'

He puts both hands together and Danny places his left foot in them.

'Ready?' Zamora says. 'Just like voltige. On three . . .'

Danny reaches up as the dwarf propels him to the ceiling, making a grab for the release lever – and the ladder comes rattling down, nearly braining them both.

Danny scrambles up the metal rungs, bangs open the trapdoor and finds himself in blinding sunlight on the Mansions' roof, gulping good clean air. Zamora follows him up, coughing furiously.

All of Kowloon, the harbour, the island, lie spread out before them. Perpendicular lines of the skyscrapers cut the curve of the hills beyond. A dizzying world.

To the right there's a smart office block, the same height as the Mansions. It's tantalizingly close across a narrow – but lethal – twenty-four-floor drop. A gust of wind sweeps the rooftop, stirring the rubbish and weeds, and then dies again.

'*Caracho!*' Zamora blinks at the view. He turns quickly back to the trapdoor, but bullets come zipping up the stairwell and he ducks away. 'Give me a hand to barricade this or we're done for.'

Danny's eyes scour the rooftop. Maybe there's something big to heave over the trapdoor, but then what? Any other way off? The asphalt roof is covered in rubbish: old TVs, lampshades, plastic chairs, a tangle of aerials and wires . . . nothing useful. And no other doorways. But then he spots something else glinting in the sunlight, and runs over to it.

A tall metal ladder lies amongst the weeds, slowly being throttled. The idea springs to mind in one clear inspiration – and puts him in motion before he has time to think it properly through. Tugging the thing free from the tangled plant growth, he drags it to the narrow chasm at the far side of the roof. Cautiously he edges to the very brink.

Far below he recognizes the alleyway where he hypnotized Pony Tail at the bottom of a gut-wrenching drop. He eyes up the ladder – it should just span the distance from this roof to the next. It looks sound enough. Aluminium or something like that. No rust and definitely in one piece.

He stands it up vertically, judging the gap, struggling against the wind which is gusting again – and then lets it fall across the chasm, one foot anchoring the bottom rung.

Just forget the drop, Mum would say. *It's only as real as you allow it to be. On the wirewalk nothing else exists but the wire, and the wire is there to hold you up. It's your friend, Danny.*

'Major!' he calls, looking back to where – wreathed in smoke – Zamora's struggling to close the trapdoor. The dwarf looks up questioningly. It's only as Danny takes in the backdrop behind that he realizes there's a problem: Zamora's profound vertigo.

He's already waving his hands in front of him as he picks his way across the roof, guessing the worst. 'It's no use saying "don't look down", Danny. I can't do it. No way, nooo way.' For the first time during the last twenty-four hours he looks scared. 'No, I'll take my chances in a straight fight with those boys. You save yourself. And find Miss Laura.'

There are voices behind him now and a head pops up through the trapdoor. A long arm extending, aiming a pistol in their direction. Danny calculates the possibilities. Leave Zamora behind? Unthinkable. I need his solidity. Strength. But it's unlikely he's going to get across the chasm either. He imagines wandering the sprawling metropolis on his own . . .

'I'll be just fine,' Zamora is saying, glancing over his shoulder.

'No time to argue!' The wind's gusting again, ruffling Danny's quiff. 'They've got guns. Dad would want you to do it! Just follow me.'

He turns back to the drop and eyes the rungs of the

ladder. He's walked slack wire before. And been on the practice rig for tightwire. Barely above the ground. Never had the inclination or courage to go much higher. That was Mum's domain – *you need the height*, she would say, encouraging him to give it a go. *You need the height to feel things matter.*

He's never done anything like this.

Despite himself he glances down and immediately feels the drop pulling, as if it's hungry for him. He remembers watching the grainy YouTube video of the legendary Karl Wallenda falling to his death from the skyscrapers in Puerto Rico. Over and over again.

He breathes deeply.

Nothing but the wire. He takes another breath, lets it out slowly and then he's taken that first step, onto the ladder, holding his arms straight, softening his knees, feeling it solid against the soles of his shoes. Must make it look easy for Zamora, he thinks. Place one foot, then the next, then the next.

Just a short walk, as if the ladder's on the ground. He frees his right foot from the safety of the roof. The first step establishes the rest – it's the one you need to get right. In his peripheral vision the void gapes below, and then he realizes something. Even if they weren't running for their lives, there's something irresistible about taking that step. It can't be denied.

Here we go. Left, right, left. Steady. He uses his arms to balance a wobble and waits for a second as the wind twists around him, poised midway across the chasm.

Need to trust my centre of gravity. Take time to balance. The wind drops again. For a fleeting moment, he feels a kind of bounding elation, feels vital, alive – fully alive! He looks around at the vastness of the city, eyes wide open.

And then he's away again.

It takes five more quick steps, treading with purpose on each rung. There's just his feet and the ladder and nothing else, not a single stray thought, and then he feels the gritty surface of the next rooftop and his knees suddenly threaten to buckle. Another deep breath steadies him and he turns to look back, the blood singing in his veins, tingling all over.

A gunshot shatters the glory of the moment.

'Come on, Major!' Danny shouts, putting strength into each syllable. 'You can do it. Head high.'

The dwarf hesitates, puffs out his cheeks. Takes a breath, and then half a hesitant step towards the edge. He stops. He's not going to be able to do it, dammit!

Another gunshot. Figures on the roof running towards the Major.

'For God's sake, Major. Call yourself a showman! I've seen braver jossers!'

That does it. The dwarf crosses himself three times, taps the bowler hat firmly onto his head – and takes a shaky step onto the ladder, then another. He puts out his arms resolutely to either side, fingers splayed.

The gang members are scrambling across the roof, angry shadows in the billowing smoke.

'Keep looking at me,' Danny calls. 'Trust your feet.'

The wind gusts again, and Zamora reaches up to hold his bowler. He wobbles.

'Forget your stupid hat. Keep your arms working!'

Danny ducks as another gunshot zips over their heads. And then Zamora virtually breaks into a run, the ladder chattering under his heavy tread, bouncing dangerously – and he's standing with Danny, astonished. He opens his mouth but nothing comes out, and instead he turns and gives the ladder an angry kick, sending it tumbling, clanging off the air-con units and fire escapes, down into the alleyway below. It's a hellish fall and Zamora regrets the seconds he spends watching it go, his stomach knotting.

'Let's go, Major!'

They're on a roof garden amongst pot plants, benches, sunloungers. A woman in a business suit sits up on one of the reclining chairs, staring at Zamora and Danny as they hurdle a low barrier and charge towards an access door.

'*Bon dia*,' Zamora says, tipping his bowler. 'Hope you enjoyed the show.'

Danny glances back to see Triad members running towards the chasm, and then he and Zamora are in the stairwell, down a flight of steps, through a deserted boardroom, the bright hum of an open-plan office – and straight into a waiting lift.

Zamora thumps the ground-floor button so hard it nearly implodes. 'God. I think I'm going to be sick,' he says, steadying himself against the lift wall.

Unlike the lift in the Mansions this one's smooth and fast, and they plummet the twenty-four floors almost as fast as the ladder.

Out on the pavement Danny squints back up towards the roof of the Mansions. Black smoke is smudging the air and a tiny figure peers down at them, pointing. Faintly you can hear him shouting, but the words are lost.

There's a siren approaching at speed.

'Taxi!' Zamora calls, and pushing past a confused backpacker propels them both onto its waiting seat.

16 HOW TO FEEL ANGRY

The metropolis glides by drenched in sunshine.

Danny sits back and realizes his legs are shaking as the adrenalin goes thumping through his system, excitement muddling itself with disappointment, fear, the elation of being poised high over the drop.

Something else is there too.

If only Dad could have seen the muscle reading. If only Mum could have seen me on the ladder . . . If only. It's a voice he can't usually hear – and when he has heard it whispering he has suppressed it.

Yes, he has felt the shock, the grief. And, yes, he has felt the crushing guilt at surviving the fire, that he selfishly ran away that evening, driven by some childish tantrum, some need for attention. But now he feels anger – the anger that has been lurking there, ever since the tragedy.

How could they have left him alone? How on earth could they have allowed themselves to be burned up by the fire? How could they have been so careless? And left him without the Mysterium, locked up half comatose in Ballstone, or fighting for his life on a rubbish-strewn roof halfway across the world?

What the hell were they thinking?

He leans back on the seat, eyes closed. No point being overwhelmed by that now. He remembers the rain hammering on his face outside the Bat – stimulating, tingling – how it cleared his head. I am waking up, he thinks. And when I ran out across that ladder I felt like I used to in the Mysterium. Fully awake and not just waiting for life to start happening again.

He opens his eyes, the colours there glowing intently as his thoughts race on. Now I'm awake, I know what I need to do. Find Laura, of course. But more than that – I need to go back and do what I should have done that long year and a half ago. I need to find out what really happened to Mum and Dad. Find out why and how they were taken away. Find out what they both kept tight to themselves. Open up the past and peer inside at all of the stuff lurking there – good *and* bad. Reveal it. Face it.

The dwarf has been watching him closely.

'OK, lad?'

'Yes. I'm fine.' His voice is calm, focused.

'Perhaps we should go back to the police?' Zamora says.

'No. Think about Lo typing the wrong thing. We can't trust him.'

'And you said he got those Chinese characters wrong. We could try to find this other detective. Tan.'

'If Laura can't find him, I doubt we can.' Danny looks the dwarf full in the face. 'You never said you'd pocketed that gun.'

'Thought it might come in handy. But I'd never shoot. Not my style.'

'You were expecting trouble, weren't you? From the start?'

'There's always trouble,' the dwarf says heavily. 'Besides, I wasn't the only one to pocket something at the crime scene, was I?'

Danny slumps back on the seat, considering. His heartbeat's coming back down the gears and the nausea subsiding.

'What's done is done,' Zamora says. 'Right now we've got work to do.'

'You're right,' Danny says. 'And we've got more to go on now. I found a note from Aunt Laura on the wall at the gym. It said CHEUNG CHAU. That's two references we've got to it. And then it said, LOOK FOR WHITE SUIT BE CAREFUL. So she does know about him – or saw him after she was kidnapped.'

Zamora rubs his bald head thoughtfully. 'It could mean, "be careful of White Suit". Or "find White Suit, and be careful". Let's go back to the hotel and see if there's any messages. Then we could ask Kwan about getting to this blasted island.'

Once again Danny does his best to force the image of boltcutters and severed fingers from his mind. He leans forward to the driver. 'Pearl Hotel, please. And a bit faster?'

The neon signs are pale in the daylight. One of them says: HONG KONG: It's an AMAZING Adventure!

'Too blooming right,' Zamora says. 'And I'm a middle-aged dwarf now. Should be putting my feet up, *no*?'

Danny's attention is drifting. He's thinking again about the lipstick gash, the dead fish, the red-painted water tank. There is *some* kind of a link, he thinks. It'll come if I relax. But that's easier said than done with the adrenal system still pumped by the ladder walk.

Finding Laura is the pressing problem, but for some reason his mind won't stop working back to the failed

Water Torture Escape.

'Major? Dad *was* good at what he did, wasn't he?' he says suddenly.

Zamora looks taken aback. 'Good?! One of the best, Danny. As good as I've seen. The burning rope. Hypnosis. The escape stunts. All worked to look new and modern and cool . . . not a workaday grifter like Jimmy Torrini. No, your mum and dad were the real deal, Danny.'

'So why did the water torture go wrong?'

'I don't know. I just don't know.' Zamora rasps the stubble on his head. 'We had it smooth as silk every day in rehearsal. Not much that *could* go wrong really. I checked the equipment over the next morning. All fine.'

'But Dad didn't make mistakes—'

'Hardly ever. He said he learned from when Houdini got it wrong – when he was impetuous and didn't plan things properly. Heart ruling head.'

'And don't *you* think it's odd that the fire happened so quickly afterwards?'

'It certainly felt weird at the time. Didn't feel right in my bones . . .'

At last! Someone actually acknowledging the feeling he's had all along. Danny's heart picks up its beat again. 'I knew it! It always seemed wrong!'

'Maybe. But one thing at a time, eh? Just like your dad did. Lock by lock.'

The taxi slips down into the tunnel of the Eastern Harbour Crossing and they're swallowed by the gloom. The Major glances at his young friend. 'I'll tell you one thing though, my lad. He and your mum would have been very proud of you indeed today.'

Danny turns away. Zamora's words smart like lemon juice in a cut and suddenly tears are swelling his eyes – some of the few he's allowed himself since the night of the fire. He looks out at the passing tunnel walls and the tunnel lights blur and pulse.

'We're going to find Laura,' Danny says. 'That's the priority. And then I'm going to find out what really happened at the Mysterium.'

When they come back up into the daylight he's already wiped the tears away – and a renewed determination is dancing in his eyes. Zamora pats him on the shoulder and looks away, fighting his own emotion.

'I'm with you, Danny. I'm right with you wherever you want to go.'

17 HOW TO ORDER UNUSUAL ROOM SERVICE

Back at the Pearl they ride the lift to their room, each locked in silent thought. No news of any kind waits for them in the lobby. The lack of communication seems ominous.

'I reckon we should clear out,' Zamora says. 'The Dragon know this is where we're based. And I'd rather not hang about and discover whether Lo or Chow are on our side or not. And White Suit or Pony Tail could find us if they're on the loose.'

'We should head for that island,' Danny says. 'Laura must have known she was going there. Or she wouldn't have written it so forcefully.'

'I'd have thought your embassy might have touched base at least,' Zamora says. 'Let's give Kwan a call. Get him to take us to Chop Suey island or whatever the hell it's called.'

The taxi driver's phone is switched to a voicemail

message in Cantonese and Zamora leaves a message to call them back as soon as possible.

'We'll give him thirty minutes. Should be safe till then. Which is just enough time to stoke up.' He picks up the room service menu. 'That's good strategy. The circus marches on its stomach we used to say.'

While Zamora places a long and very precise order with the desk, Danny takes out Laura's notebook, flipping rapidly through the pages. On the penultimate page of the notes there's a roughly drawn table with three columns. The first is obviously a list of dates ranged back over the last twelve months or so. The second, a list of what look like names: The Yangtze, Grasshopper, The Hummingbird, Kanamaru.

The third column is headed 'Carrying' and the scribbled entries below include: Bauxite, Electrical Goods and Unknown. Some words have red lines drawn through them. Must be boats and their cargo? But why would Laura be interested in that?

The last date is just a week or so ago. The name is unreadable, but the cargo is clear: TOXIC WASTE? A strong tick is next to it. Danny unfolds the newspaper clipping with the picture of Chow on the waterfront.

'I ordered you egg fried rice, prawns and extra

noodles,' Zamora says, looking over Danny's shoulder. 'Sound good?'

'Yeah. Great,' Danny says absently. 'Maybe Chow's OK after all. What do you make of Sing Sing, Major?'

'Feisty. Bit full of herself.'

'But she's on our side, don't you think?' he hedges. 'Not against us surely.' But how much of that is wishful thinking, heart trying to out-think the head?

A smart knock at the door makes them both jump.

'Food,' Zamora says, rubbing his hands together. 'That was quick.'

He pads across the carpet and whips the door open – to be greeted by White Suit.

The man's standing there with a half-smile lifting his long face. He doesn't wait to be invited in, but brushes past the surprised dwarf, his hand reaching into his inner jacket pocket.

'Close the door, please, Major Zamora. I should like to have a little word with you both.' His voice is flat, calm, just a trace of a French accent.

'Keep away from the boy! Who on earth are you?'

White Suit walks over to Danny and snaps open his wallet to reveal an ID. 'Inspector Ricard. Interpol, Hong Kong bureau. Pleased to meet you.'

Danny takes the wallet in his hands and checks

the photo against its owner. The thing looks authentic at any rate. 'What do you know about Laura's kidnapping?'

'Not much more than you, Danny. And I need to tell you that I have been unable to persuade the Hong Kong police not to press charges. Against you both.'

'Charges?'

Ricard counts them off, one finger at a time. 'Criminal damage, tampering with a crime scene, removing items from said crime scene, trespass, assault. More recently, grievous bodily harm, trespass and arson. Heavens, *mes amis* – I'm running out of fingers!'

'But that's ridiculous!' Zamora explodes.

'Of course it is. It's a ridiculous world, *n'est ce pas?*'

'Hang on, Major.' Danny holds up a hand, studying Ricard intently. 'Can you tell us why you were following us from the airport?'

'Just keeping an eye.'

'And the kidnapping?'

Ricard looks him up and down and nods, as if he too is checking Danny against some internal information.

'Black Dragon. No doubt about it. It's odd that we haven't had the ransom demand yet. I imagine we'll have that soon enough.'

'Aunt Laura doesn't have much money. I don't know who would pay it.'

Both grandparents on Dad's side died when he was very young. Isn't there an uncle out in Canada? Danny's not sure. The man could well be dead too. Laura is his only family.

'I expect there's ways and means,' Zamora says. 'We could get in touch with the Circus Benevolent Fund. I don't know.'

'Do you have much money, Major?'

'Me? *No, señor.* Not a huge fortune to be made in our racket. You know that.'

Ricard crosses to the window, looking down at the street. 'We may have to get a bit of a move on, my friends.' He frowns. 'The police have just arrived.'

'But aren't you the police?' Zamora says.

'Different kind.'

'How do we know we can trust *you?*' Danny says.

Ricard looks him full in the eyes. 'If you're anything like your father, Danny, you should be able to peek inside my head and see there's nothing for you to fear. Go on. Take a good look.'

'What do you know about Dad? What's going on?'

There was something about the way Ricard's face relaxed as he mentioned Dad though. Danny saw that so often in the Mysterium, how his father could stroll into a fraught rehearsal and clap someone on the back, give a word of encouragement and, hey presto, the mood was softened.

'I know that he liked to make people smile.'

That was true enough. After all, Dad was the kind of man who couldn't fry three eggs without juggling them first – just for what he called the *'frisson of catastrophe'*.

'And I know that he was a decent judge of character,' Ricard adds. 'As, I'm sure, are you.'

'OK,' Danny says, making his decision. 'OK. We'll do what you say.'

The tall man smiles. He hands Danny a small card. 'Grab what you need to lie low for a couple of days, and follow me. I'm going to show you the emergency exit. Make your way to this address. It's my flat in Tsim Sha. Key's obvious enough for a smart guy like you. Look out for a bit of luck. You'll be safe enough there while I try to work out what's what . . .'

Danny scrutinizes the card: INSPECTOR JULES RICARD. INTERPOL. HONG KONG, it says. The bureau office address has been struck through, and underneath it, in an elegant hand, is another address: Flat 42, Preston Villas, Tsim Sha.

'What about Lo? Is he someone we can trust?' Zamora asks, picking up his bowler, casting a longing look at the menu lying on the table.

'Lo?' Ricard says. 'Maybe not.'

'And what about this other detective Miss Laura wanted to talk to?'

'I'm afraid to say that Detective Tan is probably dead,' Ricard says, very deliberately picking a short black hair from the sleeve of his suit. 'That's the stakes we're dealing with here. Very high. Now, come on gentlemen. It'll be much harder for us all if you're sitting in a cell. So what's it to be?'

Ricard takes a step backwards, giving Danny space in which to think. That feels good. He's not pressurizing me. Letting me make my own mind up.

'OK.' He glances back at Ricard. The worst thing to do now would be to lose momentum. Get pulled back into that frozen state, unable to act.

Danny grabs his rucksack and shoves in a change of clothes, Laura's notebook. At the last moment he swipes his cards off the bedside table and joins Zamora by the door.

Ricard holds his finger to his lips. 'Let me take a look.' He opens the door very quietly. At the far end of the corridor the lift machinery is already purring, numbers ticking off the floors.

'Quick!' Ricard says, leading them the other way down the corridor. 'Whatever happens they mustn't see me with you . . .'

'Do you mean the police? Or the Dragon?' Danny says.

Ricard ignores him. They have come to a polished steel hatch in the wall marked 'Laundry Chute'.

'Your emergency exit, gentlemen,' Ricard says, and the half-smile is back on his face.

'You can't be serious,' Zamora says. 'We'll be turned to mush.'

'And this from a star of the Mysterium?' Ricard says. 'This from the intrepid Captain Solaris?'

'How on earth—'

'Your reputation precedes you, my friend. I hear you were quite wonderful!' He opens the laundry chute and steps back, glancing down the corridor. 'We have about ten seconds to spare.'

Zamora takes a deep breath. 'I'll go first, Mister Danny. As a wise man once said, I didn't worry about being born, so why worry about dying!'

He doesn't sound convinced, but puts one foot, then the other into the black throat of the chute. 'If I can walk across that ladderrrrr . . .' He pushes off and is gone in an instant.

As Danny works his own feet into place, two sheets from a higher floor go swishing past. Flickering ghosts in the gloom.

'I'll see you later tonight,' Ricard says – and gives him a shove in the small of the back. '*Bon voyage!*'

Gravity swallows Danny and he drops like a stone.

18 HOW TO MAKE AN EMERGENCY EXIT

The acceleration is terrifying. The polished sides of the chute propel him downwards, wind whistling in his ears, a rushing sound from below and a distinct thump and groan as Zamora's knocked from side to side.

The shaft kinks one way, then the other. He bumps an elbow hard, then takes a glancing blow to the back of his head that makes stars dance in his eyes. He hurtles past another open door to see the face of a cleaner flash past, staring in wide-eyed disbelief.

There's a long, drawn-out cry of 'Gerrrrronimooo!' from below, then a thud as Zamora hits the bottom. The last few moments are the worst. The laundry chute makes two sharp twists, knocking the wind out of his lungs, and he hurtles full pelt into the waiting skip-sized laundry basket, landing in a confusion of sheets and pillow cases and towels and arms and legs, slamming into the half-buried Zamora.

There's a groan. And then silence for a long moment.

'Are you OK, Major?' Danny says, checking his own body to make sure that everything's moving properly.

'*Madre de Dios,*' the dwarf groans, struggling to come up for air. 'That's worse than the cannonball, I can tell you. And where's my bowler?'

Seventeen floors above their heads, Ricard stands in the corridor outside their room, watching Lo and two other detectives riffling through suitcases and drawers, throwing things over their shoulders, working fast.

'Still nothing from the kidnappers?' he calls through the doorway.

Lo looks up, pushing the thick mop of hair out of his eyes.

'They take time sometimes, Ricard. You know that.'

'And the missing boat?'

'All in hand. No problem.'

One of the other men is throwing things from Zamora's case. He stands up, a big grin on his face now, holding a bag of white powder in his gloved hands.

'Aha,' says Lo, feigning surprise. 'Well, nothing is ever what it seems, is it, Ricard?'

The Interpol man frowns again as Lo takes the bag of suspicious-looking powder from his inspector. 'Looks like our short friend has been doing a bit of smuggling . . . We'll throw more firepower at finding them. Got plenty to press charges now.'

Ricard inclines his head and looks at Lo. He doesn't smile back.

From where the laundry skip sits in the service basement of the Pearl, Danny can see five other large baskets, filled to the brim, standing ready to be collected.

'Let's make ourselves comfortable,' he says. 'Maybe we can get a lift out of here.'

Every now and then a soft whisper in the chute grows to a hiss, and another sheet or towel comes tumbling down onto them. It would be comical – if Laura wasn't in the hands of the gangsters, and threatened with the loss of digits or worse. If he and Zamora hadn't just run for their lives, dodging bullets on a seedy rooftop. If Mum and Dad were still alive . . .

His head still aches a bit from the bump in the chute and his thoughts are jumping from one to the next. He thinks of Laura and her predicament, which makes him think of Detective Tan and Ricard's dark assessment of the detective's fate. And that makes him think of the harbour and fish, which leads to the aquarium exploding in the Golden Bat, and that – the fishtank – brings him back again to the Water Torture Escape. And his parents and the Mysterium. Always now his thoughts are coming back to the Mysterium.

It's pulling me back, he thinks. Like gravity.

The deck of cards is in his hands, and he's working them like worry beads. Zamora looks at them snapping through his long fingers.

'Hey, Mister Danny. You were going to show me the jumping man.'

'Now?'

'We've got time, *no?*'

Danny smiles in spite of everything. He shuffles the cards, working the King to where he wants it, preparing the force, the actions relaxing him. Feels easier than it did at school. He remembers Dad doing the very same trick, sitting on the trailer's steps, one summer's evening long ago on the outskirts of Rome. First time he saw it. Some of the Aerialisques were watching and the evening breeze was ruffling the black ostrich feathers on their costumes. Someone playing flamenco guitar in the distance – and Dad's hands looked so calm, so easy as he joked with everyone. That was the life . . .

'Pick a card, Major.'

The trick goes like clockwork, the king taking a decent jump, tumbling like a 'flyer' on the trapeze, and Zamora applauds silently.

'Good stuff, Mister Danny.'

There are footsteps approaching. Voices in the corridor.

Quickly Zamora pulls the lid shut and they burrow down into the sheets.

They hear some of the other skips being wheeled across the concrete floor, and then suddenly their own basket lurches, and they're on the move themselves – spun around, shoved out through flapping plastic doors, back into the humidity and heat of the afternoon, bumped up a ramp. Sunlight chinks through the basket onto their faces.

'OK. *Vamos!*' Zamora mutters as the laundry men heave the basket onto the lift at the back of their waiting truck.

'But where to?' Danny says, tucking the cards away.

Zamora smiles, his face mysterious in the striated light, expression hard to read. 'No straight roads in this world, Danny. Just labyrinths.'

* * *

The Happy Laundry truck reverses out of the loading bay. Its smiling sun logo flashing yellow as it emerges from the back of the Pearl.

Unnoticed, it slips from the service road and merges with the mangle of traffic on Connaught Road.

It's reflected in Sing Sing's sunglasses as she sits impassively in a café across the street, mobile clamped to her ear, talking urgently in Cantonese.

It passes – without raising any attention – a squad car, where Detective Lo sits pensively, chain smoking, running a hand through his shaggy hair.

It glides effortlessly past three men waiting in a side street on their motorbikes, black-tinted visors pulled down over their faces. One of them takes off his helmet and shakes out his long slick pony tail, his back still smarting from the retribution cuts he has received from the Triad. In his eyes, the desire for vengeance.

Standing on the pavement, Ricard watches the laundry truck gliding past and tells himself that he too is doing the right thing. That it can all work out just fine. That the sun will smile on them all.

The van turns a corner and disappears from sight.

ACT TWO

Only mystery makes us live. Only mystery.

Lorca

1 HOW TO GET A TRIM WHEN KIDNAPPED

Laura comes slowly to something like consciousness.

Her head hurts like crazy and she hasn't a clue where she is. The room's dark and her vision is swimming uncertainly. Her mouth is dry and she has the nagging sensation that she might have been sick.

Must have drugged me, she thinks. Pigs.

She remembers the gym, writing with lipstick on the wall. Frantic moments that she realized it might be her only chance. As long as someone finds that message there might be a chance. Maybe even Danny?

Come off it. He's a clever lad, but still only twelve. One day he'll be as resourceful as his dad, I should think. Not yet.

Should have told Danny before. Should have written the message differently. Made it clear about White Suit. Damn and blast. But then there was only a second – and no more – to scrawl on the wall and flip the chart back. Major Zee's quite handy when the chips are down though. Wouldn't be the first time he's stepped up to the plate. What's wrong with the floor . . . ?

She gets to her feet and lurches sideways. Surely not that groggy? Now she feels the remnants of the gaffer tape on her wrists, the sore patches around her mouth. Must have trussed me like a chicken and taped my big mouth shut. Oh boy.

She staggers again in the semi-darkness. The floor's falling and rising, falling and rising. And from somewhere below comes the throb of a big diesel engine.

A door opens, a bare bulb in the corridor beyond silhouetting a man as thin as a stick, advancing into the cabin. He's got a pistol and is waving it at Laura. All spiky angles.

'Lie down. You lie down!'

'OK. I'm lying down.'

Another figure, as fat as the other is skinny. He crouches over her now waving a large pair of scissors in her face. They don't look at all clean. And the man carries an overpowering smell of fish with him that makes her gag.

'Your hair,' he says. 'Need hair now. Not move.'

'OK. You're the boss. Just a little off the length, please.'

'Shut up!' Fatty shouts, and clunks the scissors rapidly together twice. 'Or I cut something else.'

Jeepers creepers, Laura thinks. What a mess. Still, if I get out of it I'm going to have a hell of a story. Front-page stuff.

The thought gives her a tiny lift. She shuts her eyes as the scissors start snapping away close to her ear, thinking of the great copy this will make. It helps to think of something else, and to distract herself she experiments with opening sentences.

'Hey! Watch it, lardboy. That was nearly my ear.'

2 HOW TO IMPROVE YOUR LUCK

The Happy Laundry truck heads for home.

It's pitch black in the basket in the shuttered back of the van, but it's a relief, Danny thinks, not to have to make decisions for a few minutes. He closes his eyes and settles back amidst the sheets and towels, thinking about Ricard again.

Could the man be OK? The look on his face was one that has become very familiar of late. It said, I know a bit more than you do, Danny. Everyone seems to know more than me: Laura, Zamora, Sing Sing . . .

And now Ricard. As Zamora said, Laura's message on the wall could be read either way: Watch out for White Suit. Trust White Suit.

Damn it. How to know who to trust?

He remembers Dad doing the 'safety' on the escapes. *Always do your own checks, old son – you may trust everyone around you, but you only know the thing's ready if you've done it yourself.*

So what went wrong in the water torture cell? And at some point surely you have to trust someone other than yourself. So start from a firm base and work up from there. I trust Zamora. Stupid even for a moment to think there's a problem there.

He looks in the dwarf's direction. In the darkness it seems easier to ask certain questions.

'Major Zee?'

'Yes, *amigo*.'

'Who did you trust – when we were in the Mysterium?'

'Everyone. Well, nearly everyone. A couple of the temporary roustabouts gave me a bad vibe, if you know what I mean. Couple of the Khaos Klowns too. Rosa agreed with me about them.'

'No. I mean when you were doing the cannonball. Or the Wall of Death. Who did you trust to set the equipment?'

'Well, I let the riggers do most of it,' Zamora says, considering. 'But I always checked things at the last moment. That way I could only blame myself if something went wrong. Like the popcorn accident. Oversight on my part. It's a matter of responsibility.'

Danny thinks about this for a moment. Makes his decision.

'I'll take the responsibility if we're wrong.'

'Shared responsibility, Mister Danny. Tell you what though, the other person I didn't like—' The Major's about to say more but the truck slams over a speed bump, knocking the words from his mouth. They're dropping down a ramp. Danny feels his stomach rise – as if they're on a rollercoaster drop – and then the brakes are bringing them to a squealing stop.

'Last stop,' Zamora says brightly. 'Let's hop out before someone puts us on a boil wash!'

They're out of their basket and waiting when the shutter at the back of the van comes flying up. A sleepy laundry worker looks bemused at the sight that greets him. To say the least.

'What are you doing in truck?'

'What do we owe you, *señor*?' the Major beams, and hops down. 'And where are we?'

They're standing in a basement loading bay. Other Happy Laundry vans are pulled up to the raised concrete walkway at the back. The heat and noise are oppressive.

'Kowloon,' the man says. 'Shantung Street.'

'*Muchas gracias*,' Zamora says, patting the man heartily on the back. He turns to Danny, his smile fading.

'We're back across the harbour again then. What now? We could try Kwan again. See if he can come and drive us around. Cheung Chau maybe?'

Danny nods. 'OK. But first I think we should see what Inspector Ricard has to say.'

'I'll borrow the phone here,' Zamora says, bustling off towards the laundry office.

'Hurry. I'll wait for you at the top of the ramp'

Danny trots back up to the bright street. Images form in his mind, different versions of what is happening to Laura. He sees her chained and bound to a chair; locked in a tiny, airless room; trussed up in a canvas sack; curled up in the boot of a car. Dimly he's aware that all of these are versions of challenges that he saw Dad tackle and defeat – and that they probably bear no relation to the truth. But every time he sees the words *dim sum* or *chop suey* he can't help thinking of Laura chatting away gaily on the plane, and sees her finger poised in the jaws of the cutters.

Kowloon hurries past. Smart ladies doing their shopping carrying small, preening dogs, teenagers trying to look cool, businessmen with their mobiles glued to their ears, tourists hogging the pavement with semi-permanent cricks in their necks and city guides in their hands.

It's just another day for them. Strange how the world carries on as normal when your own version of it is falling apart. Danny recognizes the sensation from the interminable days between the trailer fire and the funeral. Berlin went on its way all around him. Everything – the people doing their shopping, the dogs on their leads, the market traders, the school children hurrying home – all frustratingly blind to the fact that Mum and Dad were dead and gone. The stars, hard and clear overhead.

Oblivious to his shock.

Different country, different weather – same feeling. How strange that the worlds of the ordinary and the extraordinary can live so closely side by side, divided by the thinnest of spaces. You take one step and you've slipped from one to the other. And if Laura hadn't been kidnapped then he and Zamora would be just like the other tourists looking for the next place to eat, the next sight to see and photograph. And yet that's not quite right either. The whole story – from the arrival and kidnapping to Ricard's intervention – feels as if it was bound to happen. Fate.

Zamora comes up the ramp scratching his head, blinking in the sunlight. 'Boy, oh boy. You're not going to believe this. The taxi dispatcher says Mister

Kwan's gone missing, Danny. Nobody's seen him since he dropped us at those horrible Mansions yesterday. His wife is worried sick apparently.'

Danny shakes his head. Can't be happening – it feels like a bad dream, one that just gets progressively worse as the night wears on, no matter which way you turn. 'We shouldn't have got him involved.'

'Maybe he's just gone on a jaunt? Maybe his wife's an old dragon,' the dwarf says, sounding unconvinced. 'He certainly looked stressed. Come on. We've got to focus on Laura.'

'Agreed. But let's start at Ricard's.'

'But keep our wits about us, *no?*' Zamora says firmly, stepping out into the roar of the traffic. 'TAXI!'

The taxi driver spins them back towards the tip of Kowloon. Sun and shadow whipping across them as they tick off the blocks.

'I guess they must pay these Interpol types well,' Zamora says, watching the buildings become grander, the shops and their brands more exclusive. 'Or maybe he's on kickbacks from the Triads too!'

'I don't think so,' Danny says.

The taxi is pulling up at a corner of Kowloon Park, a welcome oasis of greenery bubbling between the concrete and glass. A nameplate on the nearest building says Preston Villas.

'Six fifty,' the taxi driver says, cranking round in the seat.

'Excuse me asking,' Zamora says. 'But do you know a driver called Kwan Kar Wai?'

'Being funny?' the man says. 'How many thousand taxi drivers in Hong Kong, do you think? People come. People go. Who knows who anyone is these days, right?'

The Villas are older than the other buildings around the park. The stairwell is steeped in faded grandeur – a taste of incense mingling with the tang of floor polish, and the doorways to each apartment are decorated with potted plants, Buddha statues, welcoming mats.

It feels quiet and restrained after the hustling streets of downtown Kowloon.

'Fourth floor,' Zamora says, glancing at an apartment guide on the wall. 'Let's see what old Whitey's got up here.'

On the third-floor landing a black cat is curled in a wicker chair, eyeing them from a deep red cushion. It hisses at them. Eyes flash quick green slits in their direction. Then it settles back down to sleep.

Number forty-two leads directly off the next landing, a small brass plaque next to the door simply says: RICARD.

Zamora rattles the handle. 'Nothing doing? Shall we just wait for him?'

'He said we'd work out where the key is,' Danny says, looking around, but, unlike the other doors, Ricard's is uncluttered by statues or mats or pot plants or any of the other places you'd normally tuck a key.

The plain wooden door looks back at him defiantly.

Danny eyes the locks. One deadlock and one Yale type. Could probably tickle the Yale open given time. But the deadlock's beyond me, he thinks. Dad trained me for stage handcuffs and big chunky padlocks. Not breaking and entering. What did Ricard say? Key's obvious. You just 'need a bit of luck'.

He closes his eyes, trying to picture the moment that the Interpol man said that. He was looking down as he said it. That hair he picked off his sleeve!

Danny's away down the stairs to the floor below.

The black cat is still slumbering away on the cushion. As Danny approaches, it pops its eyes wide open and hisses again unpleasantly, hackles rising, claws extending.

'Easy,' Danny says soothingly. 'Ea-sy.'

The cat doesn't look at all at ease.

Danny drops his eyes to avoid direct contact, trying to make his approach seem less threatening, and approaches sideways. Then he reaches out quickly and taps the cat twice right on the top of its skull. It's an acupressure point; governing vessel twenty. Calms animals down if you get it right, just like Blanco did when his dog was playing up.

The cat hesitates, then lies down again as if suddenly very heavy, purring like a wind-up toy.

'Excuse me,' Danny says, and reaches under the cushion.

And sure enough, there are the keys.

The apartment is decorated in minimalist style. Simple furniture on the bare floorboards. Clean white walls with just one massive piece of calligraphy, the ink splattered where an enormous brush must have struck the paper explosively. Danny takes it in, trying to get a sense of Ricard and his world.

Despite the spare decor, it feels comfortable – the home of someone at ease with himself. With his conscience? Or could a crooked cop, a gangland boss, manage the same calm, cool atmosphere? You can imagine Ricard coming in, kicking off his shoes, making a coffee, lounging on the sofa. Putting his feet up.

'Might as well make ourselves comfortable,' Zamora says, peering into the kitchen. 'I'm still annoyed about breakfast.'

'He did say we could make ourselves at home,' Danny says.

He walks over to a roll-top desk against the far wall – and stops in his tracks.

There next to the phone, in a silver frame, is a photo of Dad and Mum.

Danny has to blink hard twice to make sure he isn't conjuring the thing from out of his imagination. From out of his need to see them. But, yes – there they stand, in costume: Dad in his natty black suit, thin red tie. Mum in a striped leotard, leaning against him as they stand on the trailer steps. It's not a publicity shot – too informal – and not a photo Danny's seen before. There's a quiet smile on Dad's face and Mum has turned to look up at him, blurring her face in the camera's blink. Danny gulps hard, shuts his eyes. Not now. It won't help.

Focus. What on earth is it doing here?

'Major! Take a look.'

'What have you got then?' Zamora says, picking out the urgency in Danny's voice and coming over. '*Madre mia!* Harry and Lily. Some time ago, by the looks of it.'

'Any idea when?'

'I guess around the time you were born. Turn of the millennium. Your trailer was new then so it can't be before. And your Mum's not pregnant – you can see that! But what's it doing here on Whitey's desk?'

Danny shrugs, pushing thoughts around in his mind. Trying to make sense of things.

'It's got to be a sign we can trust Monsieur Ricard, don't you think?'

'Yes. But then again, you thought he was being interrogated at the police station. And we only have his word about Lo.'

'But you only put a photo in a nice frame – and keep it out – if you care about the people in it. Don't you?'

Zamora nods, conceding the point.

He rustles the papers on the desk. Nothing of note lying about, just a few bills, receipts. The drawers are locked.

'What do you think, Mister Danny? Should I break them open?'

'No. We'll wait. See what he has to say.'

Zamora takes a breath.

'Well, I might just check the kitchen out then. The man said make yourself at home. *Mi casa es tu casa.* Words to that effect.'

Danny's eyes are fixed on the photo. There they stand. Caught in evening light, radiant. Relaxed. Not a clue what was coming their way. Is that what's it like for all of us? he wonders. Smiling at the camera because we don't know what's round the corner. Or can we grab control of things now and then? He takes a breath. Well, you can certainly try.

The phone breaks his train of thought, old-fashioned bell tone jangling, making him start. He waits, listening, his hand hovering undecided above it. Then the answer phone cuts in: 'Jules Ricard. Please leave a message. *Laissez moi un message, s'il vous plaît.*'

And then Ricard's voice comes again, this time live, urgent. 'Hello, Danny. If you can hear this, please pick up – hello?'

Danny grabs the phone from its cradle. 'Hello. I'm here.'

'Listen, sit tight until I get there, *oui*?'

And then before he has a chance to control the words, Danny is blurting them out: 'Why have you got a photo of my parents? Did you know them, Monsieur Ricard?'

Silence.

'Hello?'

'Danny. It's a long story. And I'd rather tell it in person. We don't have much time now. And listen very carefully to me: don't answer the door if anyone calls—'

Zamora has come to stand beside Danny, leaning in to try and hear the conversation.

'But why—'

'Listen to me. Things are hotting up,' Ricard says. 'We've had a ransom demand from the kidnappers. It's the Black Dragon all right. They've sent a big chunk of your aunt's hair. Ash blonde, oui?'

'Yes.' Danny nods. Knees have gone a bit wobbly. But at least it's just hair for now, not fingers. 'How much? The ransom?'

'Ridiculous amount, Danny—' Ricard pauses, coughs at the other end of the phone. 'Off the scale. But more than that they've put out a reward amongst the other Triads. For you and Zamora.'

'For us? Why?'

'Don't worry. Just keep out of sight. These gangs have a lot of members, but their organization and

186

communication is quite loose. And they don't all get on. None of them like Black Dragon much. Still, best to be on the safe side.'

'We're trying to get hold of Mr Kwan.'

'So are we. And Lo's on the warpath too. He knows someone tipped you off at the Pearl. I've got to play a careful game, Danny. They have a saying here: "Black Dog gets rewarded, White Dog gets punished." It means that things aren't always fair. And that good dogs need to be very careful.'

Things aren't always fair. Danny looks at Dad smiling back at him from the photo. 'You'll tell me about Dad? Mum?'

'Later. I promise. Well done finding the key. Knew you would. Spike can be vicious if he doesn't take to you.' He laughs. 'Did you see that scar on Lo's face! Look, one more thing.' His voice falters, for the first time betraying something other than resolute optimism. 'I'm sorry to say we don't need to waste any time trying to find Detective Tan. They just pulled his body out of the harbour. A hundred cuts, the medical examiner says. *Mon Dieu!* It's just like the old days. Don't answer that door. Wait for me.'

'Monsieur Ricard—' But the line has gone dead.

Danny stands there for a moment, the receiver

clutched in his hand, imagining Tan's body trailing blood in the murky waters of the harbour, sinking slowly to the bottom.

And then a furious hammering breaks on Ricard's front door.

3 HOW TO RISK YOUR LIFE

Danny holds his finger to his lips and crosses the floor on the lightest feet he can manage. He motions Zamora to draw the curtain – that way it won't be obvious when he takes a peep through the spyhole and blocks the light.

Zamora nods and moves to darken the room.

One more burst of knocking. But less sure now. Danny puts his green eye to the peep hole, and sees Charlie Chow standing in the hall.

The man's face looks dark as ever, but stormier. An effort to mask the emotion playing there, but there's anger for sure. His right hand is clenching slightly, unclenching. He's a little out of breath. A bit more than you'd expect from three flights of steps.

Danny turns to Zamora and mouths the words 'Charlie Chow'. The dwarf raises his eyebrows.

Chow steps back from the door and hits the touchscreen on his mobile. He cocks his head sharply, listening. The phone behind them on the desk starts ringing again.

The answer phone clicks in again. 'Jules Ricard. Please leave a message. *Laissez—*'

Chow snaps his phone shut irritably and shoves it in his pocket. He didn't dial the full number, Danny thinks. Must have had the number stored. Or he's replying to Ricard. So they know each other for sure.

The man stares at the door again, as if defying it – and then stumps away down the stairs. He's got a jiffy bag in his hand, and he shoves it into a jacket pocket as he goes.

Danny makes up his mind. 'Come on, Major. We're going to follow him.'

'You sure about that?'

'We'll see where he goes. Then come back to meet Ricard.'

'You heard what he said. About Triads, Danny. I'm responsible for you—'

'Shared responsibility, remember? We'll keep to public areas. It's broad daylight, after all.'

Zamora jams his hat back on his head. 'Well, I'd rather be doing something than sitting here twiddling my blinking thumbs.'

Danny takes a piece of paper from the desk and scribbles on it: Back very soon. Danny.

They merge into the thick crowd in Tsim Sha. Chow is just about visible ahead – his burly form parting the crowds as if he owns the very pavements. A big shark amongst small fish, top of the foodchain.

Zamora grabs a free copy of the *Hong Kong Standard* from a stall as they go.

'Camouflage. Come on, we'll lose him in a mo.'

Chow marches along, looking neither left nor right. Not once does he glance over his shoulder. Danny keeps watching him. He'd look round wouldn't he, at least now and then, if he thought he was in any danger himself? And he's going towards something, not away from something. Pulled, not pushed. More hunter than hunted? It's hard to say.

Zamora, seeing Danny's focus on Chow, takes up the guard, scanning the pavement for trouble, watching each scooter or parked car with care.

Chow crosses against a pedestrian light, oblivious to the oncoming traffic, and Danny and Zamora have a scramble to get across the road themselves, keeping their quarry in sight, dodging taxis and delivery vans.

'Let's close it up a bit, Major. He's not looked round once.'

The big man turns into a side street, then makes a fade left, moving at speed, his jacket flapping, before suddenly ducking right into a camera shop.

'He's on to us,' Zamora says.

'No. I think he's going through the motions. Just in case.'

They enter the bright interior of the shop, disorientated a moment in the sharp lights, mirrored displays. Chow is jogging heavily towards a door at the rear.

Danny and Zamora whisk across the polished floor and follow him out the same way, through the corner of a congested mall and out again, just in time to see Chow march onto an escalator, and disappear into the underground MTR system. The sign overhead says, TSUEN WAN line, Hong Kong Island.

'I wonder if we're heading towards the bad guys,' Zamora puffs. 'Or even your aunt?'

'Only one way to find out,' Danny says. 'Keep following. To wherever he's going.'

The station concourse is crowded. Chow has slowed, presumably sure he has done enough to fox anyone who might be tailing him. Who does he think might be following him, Danny wonders. Not us, surely. More likely it's other Triads. Or the cops. He watches as Chow wafts a card over the reader at a barrier and strides through.

'Tickets!' Zamora says, fumbling in his pocket for change and squinting hard at the machine, trying to work out the system.

'No time, Major.'

Danny swipes a couple of discarded tickets from the floor. Brushes the dust off them against his trousers. 'Come on.'

He strides up to a bored-looking guard on one of the gates. No time to waste. Look into my eyes, right into them. That's it. Weird to see two colours, isn't it? Distracting.

'We just bought these and they won't work on the barrier.'

The man looks down at them, but Danny moves them in a quick tight circle. 'They're good!' he says, nailing the tone with a chopping motion from his hand on the barrier.

The guard blinks, nods. Then opens his gate and waves them through.

Zamora chuckles to himself as they hoof it down the descending escalator, but there's no time to dwell on the success. Chow's out of sight on the packed escalator . . .

They hustle past the commuters, pushing past bulging shopping bags . . .

. . . And at the bottom there's no sign of him. They can hear the hiss of an approaching train, the hot breath of wind surging through the station. There's not much time.

'Which platform? North or South?' Zamora shouts over the noise, glancing at the line information on the wall.

'The Island,' Danny says. 'South.'

'How do you know?'

'Just a guess.'

The train comes thumping out of the dark maw of the tunnel alongside the crowded South platform. Danny jumps up onto a bench and, amidst the jostle, catches a glimpse of Chow boarding a carriage at the far end of the train.

'Got him, Major!'

He jumps down and pushes through the crowds, with Zamora following close behind. They're just a carriage away from the end of the train when the alarm sounds and they duck through the sliding doors in the nick of time.

* * *

The train pulls speed from the rails, diving under the harbour, back towards Hong Kong Island.

Catching his breath, Danny stares out at the dark tunnel walls. It seems that Mum or Dad or both of them must have known Ricard personally. But if so, how? And if Chow has come calling on Ricard, does *that* mean the Triad-turned-businessman can be trusted? It's like one of those Venn diagrams in maths. There's a circle for 'trustworthy' and one for 'dangerous'. He can be fairly sure that Ricard belongs in the first one and believes – hopes – that Sing Sing sits there too. And Tan would be there if he was alive. Pony Tail and the Black Dragon are in the second one obviously. But how big is the overlap? Who is in that shady area in the middle?

He shakes his head. An announcer rattles off a burst of Cantonese. Then English: '*Next station: Admiralty.*'

Danny peers into the front carriage. Chow is standing near the doors.

'Is he getting off?' Zamora says as the train slows. 'I can't see.'

No. Chow's body is heavily set. Shoulders down. Energy passive. 'Not going anywhere yet.'

The doors swish open, passengers pushing to get

off, others to get on. Chow has his eyes on the floor. Then suddenly his head swings their way. Danny's been waiting for that: he just has time to flip the newspaper up covering his face. And then the train is pulling away again.

'Last stop coming up,' Zamora says. 'Central. Sure you don't want to head back to Ricard?'

'Sure. If he does spot us then we can just have it out with him on the street. Not much can happen to us if we're surrounded by other people.'

The pre-recorded announcer is calling out the stop. *'All change. All change!'*

4 HOW TO HIDE IN EXOTIC UNDERWEAR

The crowds in Central are even heavier, and they take the chance of closing right up behind Chow as the escalator carries them back to the surface, the muggy air wrapping itself tight around them again.

'Let's be very careful about this. God knows who might be hanging around here,' Zamora says.

A police car is parked outside the exit to the station. Chow's feet hesitate for a second, and then he ducks close along the buildings, shielding himself from the patrolmen with the other pedestrians. So he's wary of the police. What does that mean? If he's dodging the good ones then that makes him suspect. If he's trying to hide from the 'bent' ones, then he could be in with the 'trustworthy'.

Whatever happens they mustn't lose him now. Need to make sure we're not seen by the police, Danny thinks.

There's a raucous teenage school group coming towards them down the street and, as the boys jostle past the subway exit, Danny tugs Zamora by the sleeve, manoeuvring them in amongst the noise and good humour. One of the boys swipes the dwarf's bowler and tries it on, laughing. Safely shielded in the group they allow themselves to be swept past the squad car and around the next corner.

Chow is still in sight as they detach from the push–pull of the teenagers. Zamora snatches back his hat and they hurry to close on Chow as he turns inland. Above them now the Peak rears up above the skyscrapers, its lush summit towering over the harbour.

Chow jinks right on one corner and then left on the next. And then suddenly his feet change their rhythm, hesitating, skipping a beat. As if he's about to turn around.

'In here,' Danny hisses, simultaneously pulling Zamora through a shop doorway – just as Chow spins round on his heels.

The assistant in the exclusive lingerie shop eyes them quizzically as Danny and Zamora hover in the doorway, peering between the frilly bras on a rack.

'Can I help you, gentlemen, Perhaps something for lady in your life?'

'Er, no thanks,' Danny says, surveying the racks of underwear with some alarm. 'Come on, Major.'

'Reminds me of the Aerialisques' trailer!' Zamora says nostalgically, hesitating for a moment – and then he hurries after Danny. 'Wait up . . .'

When they catch sight of Chow again he's moving towards a curved building that sits squat on the next corner. His pace is slowing, as he gathers his solidity around him. A ray of sunlight splashes on the sign, picking out the words: HONG KONG PEAK TRAM.

The tramway itself runs at an improbably steep angle away up the hillside, cutting between the buildings, dodging under a flyover and twisting out of sight. High above, the Peak soars against the wind-torn clouds.

But Danny's attention is snared by a small figure sitting on the station steps. It's Sing Sing.

His first thought is of how pleased he is to see her, and he almost calls out her name. But then he hesitates. We want to see what Chow's up to, after all. And maybe we don't want him to see us.

And something more. Sing Sing has set her shoulders tight in a defensive posture. She's not feeling at ease. He watches her carefully now as Chow approaches. Her head is buried in some kind of manga, trying to look like she's not waiting for someone. But her left foot is tapping away at the stone steps, all her anxiety focused into that one part of the body.

'Let's watch what happens,' Danny says, slipping into the shadow of a doorway.

Sing Sing looks up at Chow, who does no more than nod in greeting before reaching inside his jacket. He takes the envelope and gives it to her, talking quickly. Sing Sing nods twice, then thrusts the jiffy bag away in her rucksack, the big sunglasses still cloaking her eyes.

The firm line of her mouth gives nothing away as she watches Charlie Chow turn, step out into the road and hail a taxi. She waits impassively until Chow is safely in his cab, then tosses her manga away into a bin and turns to stride into the Peak Tram Terminus.

Danny's eyes follow her until she's out of sight, then move to see Chow's cab negotiating its way into the traffic. There are three options: follow Chow, follow Sing Sing or split up and follow them both.

'What do you think?' Zamora says, clearly computing the same choice.

'Follow the envelope. That's more important than who's carrying it, I reckon.'

'Could be misdirection. Like when magicians want people to look one place so they don't look another—'

Danny shakes his head. 'That envelope's heading to someone. We need to find out who. We'll keep on Sing Sing's tail.'

Zamora's watching Danny's face closely. He smiles: 'Hey, Mister Danny. You're not developing a bit of a fancy for old Sing Sing, are you now?'

'No!' Danny blushes. 'It's not that. But there's something about her. Can't quite figure it out yet.'

'You know what the philosopher said, Mister Danny. "Everything about woman is a riddle". At least to us poor *hombres*.'

There's no rush now. Only one place Sing Sing can be heading: Victoria Peak by way of the crazy angle of the incline railway.

Danny and Zamora hang back and buy their tickets at the last moment as the red carriages of the tram rumble into the bottom station. Sing Sing's up near the head of the queue, and gets a prime seat at the top of the sloping carriages, facing resolutely away up the steep tracks. She doesn't see Danny and Zamora slip to the back and open their newspaper wide, enveloped in the chatter of the tourists, the ping of their digital cameras.

'We're getting good at this cloak and dagger stuff,'

Zamora whispers as the packed tram lurches into motion. 'But give me the circus any time.'

The carriages pass under the flyover then corner hard, quickly gaining altitude, squeezing between towering buildings, flashing in and out of the sunshine. They pass within touching distance of balconies hung with washing, roof gardens littered with plastic chairs and TV aerials. Zamora looks back over his shoulder. The track drops away dizzyingly and they're already higher than some of the skyscrapers, a panoramic view of the city, the harbour slowly unfurling below. He takes a breath.

'Here we go again.'

But Danny's eyes have fallen on a story on page three of the paper. The headline barks: "Radioactive cargo ship still missing. No risk to public, say authorities." Underneath is a photograph of a heavy-jawed man staring straight at the camera. A caption says: "Contact lost with Captain Zhang Kaige and crew on Tuesday. Piracy suspected."

He nudges the Major, raising an eyebrow.

'I dunno, Mister Danny. Do you think Laura's got involved with all of that somehow?'

'It would be just like her,' Danny says.

'Wouldn't it just!'

Danny turns the pages. And right on cue there's a picture of Laura accompanying a brief piece about the kidnap. Danny skims it. Nothing he doesn't already know – but it concludes with a quote from Lo. 'We are turning every stone in the search for Miss White. But at present we have no definite leads. And we urgently need to make contact again with a relative and friend. One Danny Woo from the UK and one Mister Zamora – first name unknown.'

Danny looks at the tiny photo of Laura. They've obviously culled it from her website. He remembers taking it for her in the back garden, not long after she formally became his guardian. 'Make me look serious and intrepid,' she had said. But no matter how many they took that day they couldn't get rid of that playful gleam in her eye. 'Oh well,' Laura said in the end. 'We are what we are, I suppose.'

I wonder, Danny thinks. Wherever she is, whatever predicament she's in – I wonder if that gleam's still there in her eyes. Wouldn't surprise me. As long as she's alive. As long as they're not hacking through her little finger. Preparing the dim sum.

Despite the warmth in the packed carriages, he shudders.

5 HOW TO GET AN OVERVIEW

The tram rattles on up the wooded hillside.

The houses are spacing themselves out and are much grander, with expensive cars tucked beside them and the bright rectangles of swimming pools punctuating the lush, dark greenery. The Peak is topping out and a vast panorama unfolding.

Danny pulls his eyes from the view, back to Sing Sing. It'd be daft to lose her now. She's already on her feet, edging towards the door as they enter the upper terminus. Rucksack held tight to her side.

Through the ticket barrier, the station, through the complex of restaurants and souvenir shops . . . Danny and Zamora keep their distance from the young girl, but never allow her from sight. Her body is tense – she's trying to look calm, trying to swing her arms as if just out for a saunter on the Peak, but something's coming, Danny thinks again. Something snagging at her movements.

The wind's gusting, scudding clouds across the Peak as they emerge from the summit complex.

Sing Sing climbs up towards a viewing terrace perched above the massive drop to the city and water below, the height slowing Hong Kong's bounding pulse to a crawl.

But the view is the last thing on Danny's mind. Everything concentrated on Sing Sing's slim form. In fact, he's so intent on reading her movements – so fixed on deciphering the nuances of her body language – that it's Zamora who spots Pony Tail first.

The dwarf puts out a strong hand, blocking Danny on the steps.

'Oh boy! Our old *amigo*.'

And there's another man standing next to Pony Tail. He's got a knobbly bald head, polished by the sun like an irregular billiard ball. Cauliflower ears that look as if they've been torn and imperfectly healed more than once. A lollipop clenched between his teeth and an unbuttoned Hawaiian shirt in clashing purple and orange that flaps in the breeze.

'Bit of a looker that one, *no*?!' Zamora says dryly.

The two gangsters are lounging against a telescope, backs to the view. No attempt to blend in amongst the tourists, confident in their domain. Danny and Zamora

205

duck behind an interpretation board and peer round it as Sing Sing steps up smartly to the men.

She's waving her hand in the direction of Kowloon, talking fast. Danny tries to lip read, but it's Cantonese. No chance of working out what she's saying. What the hell's she doing talking to them? His spirits are sinking – maybe she's thick with the Dragon after all? Sliding from the good guys circle into the shady area? Or worse?

A snort of laughter from Pony Tail. Jug Ears' mouth cracks in a lopsided grin, then he draws a finger across his throat, slowly. He does it a second time, just to make sure he's getting his message across.

Who's that for, Danny thinks. For Sing Sing? Laura? Us even? Could be Tan, I suppose.

Whatever it is it makes sense to Sing Sing, who nods, setting her shoulders firmly as if facing up to them, trying to look braver than she feels. Then she reaches inside her shoulder bag and hands over the envelope. Jug Ears pockets the thing in his baggy trousers and then claps Pony Tail on the shoulder, almost knocking him off his feet. And then they're both moving, towards Danny and Zamora – straight towards them at speed.

Only one chance if they don't want to be seen.

They'll have to crouch and roll under the sign board at just the right moment. Danny holds up his hand, counting down on his fingers.

Three, two, one . . . roll!

They time it just right, flipping under the sign just as the gangsters stride past, pounding down the steps towards a parking lot. They've got what they came for, obviously – and now they're in a rush.

To get where? To Laura? Their boss maybe? So we should follow them.

Danny gets to his feet, brushing the grit from his T-shirt – and finds himself face to face with Sing Sing. She scrunches up her features in exasperation.

'Saw you two clowns on the tram,' she says matter-of-factly, a hint of a smile creeping back. 'Hope you're flipping better magician than you are a detective.'

'What was in the envelope?' Danny says, feeling deflated that she was on to them all along. Annoyed and confused too at the turn of events. He turns round, trying to see where Pony Tail and Jug Ears have gone. There's no sign of them.

'Charlie's business dealings,' Sing Sing says. 'I'm just courier girl.'

'*Caramba!*' Zamora interrupts. 'Let's keep on the trail of that blasted envelope.'

'Let it go,' the girl says firmly. 'It won't lead you to your aunt, Danny. I know that much.'

'So what the hell do you know?' Danny says, irritation punching out his words.

'That I could do with a drink. And you two need my help. Big time!'

6 HOW TO KICK SOMEONE VERY HARD

Sing Sing sips her iced coffee, then pushes the sunglasses up from her eyes. The bruise is still there – ripened by a day – plum coloured and swollen on the smooth skin. She looks Danny full in the face now. The challenging look is back, but there's definitely something softer there. Like she's reaching out.

'So. Why are you following me?'

'We wanted to see where your father went.'

'He's not my father—'

'We followed him to you. Then we followed you. We wanted to know what was in the envelope. Payment to the Black Dragon maybe?'

'Ha.' She laughs. 'Not money in there. Don't you think those Triad boys would have counted it?'

'What then?' Zamora says.

'Like I say, I'm just a messenger.'

'And what about Mister Chow? What's he?' Danny

presses, watching her face for a reaction.

'He's a good man. In difficult position. Police informer these days.'

'And what about you?' He leans back in his chair, trying to give her some space. No point pushing *too* hard. She'll just clam up.

'What about me?' She leans forward onto her elbows. Still cautious, but softening a touch more.

'What do you know about the Black Dragon?'

'Nothing much.'

That's short of the truth. Her eyes flick away briefly, one hand reaching to pull the sunglasses back down.

'Do you know where Laura is?' Zamora cuts in, tapping the metal table with a coin.

'No.'

That's true though, Danny thinks – not too fast the answer, but not too much hesitation either.

'Can you show us how to get to Cheung Chau Island?'

Sing Sing smiles. 'Sure. But you two are in *big* trouble. The Black Dragon wants a piece of you. Other Triads too.'

'We'll handle that, Miss Sing,' says Zamora.

'No offence,' Sing Sing says. 'But they'll make

mincemeat out of a couple of tourists like you.'

'Tourists!' Zamora exclaims. 'We're professional travellers, Miss Sing!'

Danny's got his cards in his hands, riffling, cutting, absent-mindedly.

'You're pretty good,' Sing Sing says, slupping the last of her drink from between the ice cubes. 'But you're carrying a bit too much tension in your shoulders.' She bumps the beaker down on the table top. Hard. 'Come on. Those two will be long gone now. We'll take a bus. But let's walk a bit first. I need to stretch my legs. Haven't been to the gym for days.'

They cross the car park, leaving the tram terminus behind, and start down the curving road that drops from the shoulder of the Peak. The greenery enfolds them, mimosa and other shrubs pungent in the humid air. The chirr of insects packing around them.

'Your mother was Chinese, right?' Sing Sing says. The tension has slipped from her body now – as if given away with the envelope – and she's moving easily down the hill.

'Yes. From here. How do you know?'

'Your aunt said. But you never been here before?'

'No. Mum went to Europe just after circus school.

Just after the handover to China. She met Dad in Italy.'

'You don't look that Chinese to me.'

Again that blunt assessment of where he does or doesn't fit!

'Maybe your dad's genes trumped your mum's?' Sing Sing goes on, oblivious, swinging her arms freely. 'You speak Cantonese?'

'Mum didn't use it much. She said she wanted to forget Hong Kong. And Cantonese wasn't her first language.'

'Can't run away from what you are.'

Always that catch in Mum's voice when he pressed for memories of her childhood and youth. 'Oh, you know,' she would say. 'Big cities can have big problems. Not much to tell. And it's all in the past.' And she would sigh and then sweep the conversation in a new direction with that fast, bright smile of hers.

Sing Sing puts a hand on his shoulder, perhaps spotting she has spoken too abrasively. '*Hou hoisam gindou neih*, Danny Woo.'

'What's that?'

'I'm pleased to meet you, Danny Woo.'

'I'm pleased to meet you too. I think.'

Sing Sing laughs.

' "I think"?! What does that mean?'

'That you keep things pretty close to your chest. There's lots you don't want to go near. I'm right, aren't I?'

Sing Sing shrugs. 'Maybe. Life is always complicated. Even more so here sometimes . . . Perhaps your mum had to deal with that.'

The light is falling on the bruise and Danny nods at it. 'You didn't tell me how you got that.'

'Didn't see the guy behind me. When your aunt was kidnapped. I should have done more. I'm sorry.'

They walk on in silence, the reality of Laura's plight hitting Danny again. It feels like someone gripping at his chest.

'We're going to find her,' he says, trying to say it confidently enough that he can feel it's a possibility, dispel the anxiety.

The road's emptier here, tourists left behind clustered on top of the Peak and the shadows deepening under the foliage. Every now and then a solitary car or small van sweeps past, but otherwise they have the place to themselves. Zamora is following a few paces behind, hands thrust in his trouser pockets. Still the warmth pressing at them and birds singing loudly from the bushes. Feels like it should be an idyllic moment

– if it wasn't for the danger waiting for them below – the urgent need to find Laura. Is it always like this, Danny thinks?

'It's weird,' he says. 'All this beauty here around us, and all the bad stuff happening at the same time . . .'

'Can't have one without the other,' Sing Sing says brightly. 'No yin without yang.'

Dimly – lost in the chain of his thought – Danny is aware that a car is approaching from behind, slowing. He just about has time to register the pricking sensation on the back of his neck, before it glides to a stop right next to them. He spins round to see Pony Tail and Jug Ears leaping from a black car, running towards them.

They look like they mean business. Pony Tail is whipping a pistol from out of his leather jacket. Jug Ears brandishing the polished barrels of a sawn-off shotgun. He takes a quick look up and down the road before advancing towards them, his holiday shirt mocking the situation.

Pony Tail snaps something out at Sing Sing in Cantonese.

'Speak English,' she says defiantly, 'so my friends can understand. And wash out your flipping mouth, toilet breath.'

Jug Ears rolls the lollipop from side to side in his

214

mouth, grins – and then meaningfully pumps a shotgun shell into the breech.

Pony Tail spits on the ground and then walks up to her. 'Get in car, Little Flower. You're in trouble. You too, short man. And you, boy, no funny stuff.'

Danny waits – taking his cue from Sing Sing who stands there, still holding her ground, hands planted on her hips.

'No way,' she says. 'Flip off.'

No one moves.

Almost as an automatic reflex Danny fingers the cards in his pocket. Ridiculously, in the heat of the moment, he finds himself thinking about which card he has on top of the deck. Ace of spades. Always know the cards, Dad would say. Be ready. You might have to do a trick on the spur of the moment. The black ace has always struck him as a powerful card with its one huge black spade stamped on it. Reassuring somehow now. He splits it from the deck.

'So? You gonna shoot us here on street?' Sing Sing snorts, jutting her jaw.

Pony Tail takes a step forward, arm straight, pistol cocked aggressively. 'Why not, Little Flower. No one around just now.'

'Don't call me Little Flower.' Gently, almost

imperceptibly, she taps Danny's trainer with her foot. 'I don't like it. And you're one ugly old Triad, Tony Flipface.'

Danny tenses his muscles, ready to react to whatever's coming. The soft contact of the shoe says, 'Get ready – something's about to happen'.

'Get in the car,' Pony Tail says, his voice flat, but waggling the pistol again for emphasis.

'OK. OK.'

Sing Sing slumps her shoulders, seemingly defeated, then, without backlift – without any warning at all – her right foot whips up and strikes hard at Pony Tail's face. The air hisses between her teeth as the kung fu kick lashes his mouth. Something cracks – like a breaking ping-pong ball – and he drops to the floor, holding his face. Jug Ears, caught off guard, hesitates, then raises the shotgun.

But it's Danny who reacts next.

The ace of spades is out of his pocket, and using a finger snap, he flicks the card – edge on – straight at the bald man's eyes. It flashes like a dart, strikes hard and true – and Jug Ears gives a yelp. He clutches an eye, letting the gun fall.

Pony Tail is struggling to his feet, the pistol still in his hands, raising it now at Danny, finger groping for the trigger. But Sing Sing's on him.

She unleashes a flurry of kicks, each thrown from a pirouette, sending him staggering back against the car, an explosive breath synching with each blow. Extraordinary force in each kick from such a slender frame, as she spins four, five times, making sure contact each time.

Zamora grabs the man's right arm as he slumps against the car, forcing it up behind his back, spilling the gun. 'You want this arm broken? Or dislocated?' he snarls. 'Your choice, *amigo*.'

Jug Ears, blinking hard, is on his feet, but before he has time to come to the aid of his partner, Sing Sing strikes the base of his neck with a firm blow and he's down, eyelids fluttering, out for the count.

Danny grabs the pistol, and hurls it into the undergrowth. A moment later it's joined by the flailing form of Pony Tail as Zamora drives him back across the pavement and, using every ounce of his strength, hurls him down the hill. The man keeps going for a long, long time, crashing through the bushes, sending birds shrieking from the trees, releasing the warm smell of crushed undergrowth as he falls.

The three victors look at each other, breathing hard.

'That was amazing,' Danny says. 'Where did you learn that?'

'From Charlie. He used to train people for movies. Five animal. Monkey paw. Drunken style. All that jazz.' She straightens her T-shirt, smoothes her hair back into place and looks at Danny. 'Your card thing was pretty damn good too, you know.'

'*M goi*,' he says, and feels pride ripple through him. The compliment means a lot, coming from this enigmatic girl. It leaves a kind of glow behind it lingering on the evening air.

Zamora's gazing after Pony Tail. 'I almost feel sorry for the poor chap. He's had a hard time of it with us. What do you say we borrow their motor?'

'I'll drive,' Sing Sing says. 'Let's get going.'

'Are you old enough?' Zamora says doubtfully.

'I'm taller than both of you. And I just saved our skins from a 426 and a 438. And anyway Charlie taught me how to drive *ages* ago.'

Danny watches her striding to the BMW, argument settled in her mind. That same lightness to her movements. She's as slim as Danny, but there's a wiry strength that belies her age and build. Training too. The kind that only comes through hour upon hour of practice and frustration. Determination. The toughened hands make sense now, and in his mind's eye he sees her striking one of those wooden sparring dummies, again and again, slowly building the muscle, hardening the skin. Ready for anything that the world might throw her way.

'I'm not arguing with you, Miss Sing,' Zamora says. 'But I'll just hide ugly chops here.'

He drags the heavy bulk of Jug Ears into thick bushes, where he rolls the man into a recovery position and then, almost tenderly, tucks his head on his crooked arm. '*Wan an*, Mister Ears.'

They drop back towards the city proper, the foliage of the Peak giving way to buildings again. The BMW smells as rank as the gym – sweat, spicy food, cigarettes imprinted on the air. Danny sits up front beside Sing Sing, while Zamora holds tight on the back seat. There's a holdall in the footwell there. He unzips it and peers in: two lengths of rope, some gaffer tape, and a meat cleaver with a ragged blade. A few strands of blonde hair on the floor beside.

Zamora surveys the contents then zips the bag shut.

'Anything interesting?' Danny says.

'Let's just say I'm sure this is the car from the kidnap.'

Sing Sing is driving quickly down the hill, expertly working the clutch and gears, using the engine to brake as they enter each sweeping curve, neatly feeding fuel to the engine as she powers out of them.

'What's a 426? 43-whatever?' Danny asks.

'Code numbers in Triad gangs. 426 is a Red Pole. An enforcer. Like a sergeant in the army. 438 is Deputy Mountain Master. Boss's number-two man. That's the guy with the ears.'

'And who's the boss?'

'I was hoping you might tell me.'

Danny looks at her as she pilots the BMW back down to sea level. Something so grown up about her. And yet something so vulnerable and young too. 'How are you mixed up in all this, Sing Sing? I mean, who are you? Really?'

'Friend of a friend. You just trust me, Mister Danny Woo.'

'I do trust you.'

Something about that hits home. Sing Sing peers forward over the steering wheel, braking hard to take a tight bend. The car fishtails and she has to steer hard to compensate.

'*M goi*,' she says.

Zamora leans forward between the seats. 'And you

can trust us. But look, Miss Sing, talking of numbers, do you know anything about the Forty-Nine?'

'No. Not much,' she says, accelerating to beat a red light, tyres thumping the tram lines. 'Criminal network. A friend of mine knows more about it.'

'And who's that then?'

'Jules Ricard. Interpol.'

Zamora and Danny exchange glances.

'We should go back to see him,' the dwarf says. 'He'll wonder where we've got to . . .'

They're passing a stationary police car and Sing Sing slows the BMW, sitting up as straight as she can in the seat.

'Not good idea right now. He's got his own problems. There's a boat hijacked.'

'The one in the papers?'

'Yep. And a couple of people are out to get him in a lot of trouble. We'll do our own thing. Head for the Ferry Pier and Cheung Chau. OK with you?'

Danny nods. 'What can you tell us about Cheung Chau?'

'It's pretty. Little fishing harbour. Very picturesque. There are no cars on it. Just bikes and scooters. And mini fire engines and ambulances. For a while a few years ago,' Sing Sing adds, weaving them into the early evening traffic, 'they used to call it Death Island.'

'Lovely,' Zamora says, leaning back heavily in his seat. 'Why?'

'People used to go there to kill themselves.'

'Super.'

They're off the Peak now. Above them the first lights are sparking the skyscrapers into night-time brilliance and the sun is dropping fast. It makes Danny think of the running sand of the hourglass video projected onto Dad's escapes.

Time sliding away.

7 HOW TO FORGET YOUR SCRUPLES

A block-and-a-half from Central Ferry terminal there's a small car park.

Sing Sing bumps the BMW up onto the pavement alongside it, clumsily straddling the kerb. She leaves the boot sticking out into traffic.

'You can drive well, Miss Sing,' Zamora says. 'But your parking's lousy.'

'I want the car to get towed,' she says. 'It'll take the Dragon longer to work out where we've gone. And it'll be safe in a police pound. Let's hurry.'

Danny gets out and – in what has now become second nature – scans their surroundings for trouble. Close by, tucked amongst the parked cars, is a red and white taxi. It looks like the hundreds of others crowding the streets, but amongst the sleek private vehicles it looks incongruous. And the dents to its side are very familiar indeed.

'Look, Major. I'd bet you anything that's Kwan's cab.'

Zamora whistles. 'That's his, all right. Same advert for teeth!'

'Who?' Sing Sing says sharply.

'A taxi driver. Drove us for a couple of days. He's been reported missing.'

Zamora trots over to it and squints in through the windows. 'Come on, Danny, how about using that toothpick of yours. Locks can't be much cop on this old thing. Doubt it's got an alarm.'

'We'll shield you,' Sing Sing says.

No time for scruples now. And maybe they can help Kwan. The lockpick is already in his hands as he approaches Kwan's car. 'I need a credit card or something like that,' he says, selecting the longer hook pick and eyeing the lock. Just the feel of the tool in his hand gives him a surge of confidence. He can imagine Dad's big hands gripping the thing and working his magic.

Sing Sing fishes in her wallet and hands him a platinum credit card.

'Charlie's. I borrow it.'

Danny's concentrating hard. He's never done this for real. Just messed around with the stage cuffs and locks under Dad's direction. But once Jimmy Torrini had shown him how to open the door of one of the vans when a drink-sodden Khaos Klown had accidentally locked both himself – and the keys – inside.

Danny probes the lock, then runs the card up the doorframe until he finds the catch. That's it, get a steady pressure there. Now give the lock a twist with the tension tool. Working both hands together the doorlock suddenly releases with a satisfying clunk. Danny pushes aside any sense of triumph and is inside in a moment, scouring the interior for anything that might give them a clue to Kwan's – or Laura's – whereabouts. There's nothing on the seats but abandoned on the handbrake is Kwan's red handkerchief. It looks forlorn.

Zamora's inspecting the outside. 'There's a parking ticket on the windshield, Danny. Today's date, but early this morning. And the wing mirror's bust.'

'That wasn't broken when we came in from the airport. I was looking in it.'

'Flat tyre too. And here on the bodywork – could be a bullet hole, *no*?'

'Then they must have got him,' Danny says, heart sinking. He thinks of Kwan's puzzled owlish face submerged in the murky harbour water, seeing nothing. Glasses broken. Gone to join Tan and his lacerated body.

'Let's get a move on,' Sing Sing says, glancing over her shoulder. 'We need Pier Five.'

The Central Ferry terminal looks like something from another age, out of place and time amidst the steel and glass of downtown. The white clock tower on the main building shows six twenty five, it's long minute hand juddering visibly.

Sing Sing rushes them under the sign for Cheung Chau and insists on buying their tickets, snapping Hong Kong dollars from a small fortune stuffed into her wallet.

Zamora raises his eyebrows. 'You're a rich girl, Miss Sing.'

'Not really. But Uncle Charlie makes sure I have enough for any eventuality. Come on, there's a fast ferry leaving. And we need to be on it.'

8 HOW TO FIND THE LADY

The jetfoil pulls away on the dot of six thirty. It slips steadily through the crowded waters of the harbour before thrusting out its powerful wake, sending them surging into open sea.

Sing Sing sits back in her seat, massaging the side of her hand. She lets out a deep breath as the safety announcements blare out. 'He had one tough flipping neck, that 438.'

Behind them the skyscrapers and Peak are shrinking rapidly against the water and sky. To the south-east there's gathering gloom, to the west pink and orange on the clouds.

'Makes me feel pessimistic if I look one way,' Zamora says thoughtfully, 'and optimistic if I look the other. Take your pick, I suppose. I might just check out the cafeteria. If you young ones will excuse me.'

Sing Sing watches him go. 'I like him. A lot.'

Danny   smiles.   Most   people   would   mention

Zamora's height – or at least do a double-take when meeting him the first time. But Sing Sing has taken the dwarf strongman in her stride, unfazed.

She looks at the cards in Danny's hands. 'So. How about that trick then?'

'I'm missing one now,' he says. It makes him feel uneasy – that deck's been with him a long time. He thinks of the cards scattering on the changing-room floor at Ballstone. How long ago *that* seems. If only sneering Jamie could see him now, what would he think?

Sing Sing reaches into her jeans pocket.

'I show you a trick,' she says, and snaps a card into the air, holding it in front of his face. 'Your card, right?'

It's the ace. A slight dent on one corner.

'I picked it up after I thumped that stupid Triad.'

'Thanks,' says Danny. 'Thanks a lot.'

'Don't mention it.'

He studies her face carefully, glad to have a few minutes with Sing Sing to himself. 'So do you live here? In Hong Kong?'

'With Chow. Since mother died. Years ago.'

'I'm sorry. How . . . did she die?'

'Killed herself. Not long after she got smuggled across from the mainland,' Sing Sing says, and turns away, as if just commenting on a small piece of bad luck or disappointing weather. But there's a hesitation in her outbreath. More emotion than she's letting on. 'Uncle Charlie adopted me.'

'And your dad?'

'He's dead too. Triad. One bad dude, people say. Nobody sorry he's dead, believe me! So – no parents left. Well, I guess you know what that feels like . . .'

She lets the thought hang. Zamora's coming back from the bar with packets of sandwiches.

'How old were you when your mum died—' Danny starts to say, but the girl just shakes her head sharply in a way that could mean anything from apology to refusal. Like he's made a bad move in chess.

'Anyone hungry then?' Zamora says, ripping the cellophane off the first pack.

'Hungry as a horse,' Sing Sing says brightly.

'Girl after my own heart, Miss Sing,' the dwarf says. 'I got you both tuna. Hope that's OK. And I've treated myself to some beer.'

Danny chews his sandwich thoughtfully and watches the water roll in the jetfoil's wake. The pulpy mouthful of bread and fish seems to have no taste whatsoever. He swallows mechanically. Need to keep strength up. Who knows what's coming next? Food and sleep have been in pretty short supply over the last thirty-six hours.

They've reached the point of no return – the Houdini point, as Dad used to call it. The moment you step from the platform onto the wire, the moment the aerialist lets herself tumble and drop, trusting the silk is knotted right to arrest the fall at the last second. The moment the escapologist plunges into the tank . . . water churning . . .

Dad flailing in the water . . .

I thought he was drowning that night. Something threw him, but he wouldn't talk about it. And when Zamora smashed the tank, and the audience saw the water gushing, I knew we were in trouble.

And there was something else. Something not right. Mum and Dad argued a couple of times that week. Very unusual that. Mum said: 'You're spending too much time with them. Something's going to go wrong.'

And Dad said: 'I've just got to do one more blasted trip, Lily. Then it's done.'

And Mum said: 'What if you get something else wrong, Harry?'

Something was worrying her, making her words ragged, her accent stronger like it always was when emotion was coursing her blood.

If I could just put a finger on it . . . the look in her eyes. In Dad's.

Sing Sing, wolfing down her own sandwich, watches him intently all the while. She swallows hard, takes a swig of water. Points at the deck of cards in his hands.

'So. Show me a trick then? Now you've got them all.'

Danny turns back from the window. He takes three cards off the top of his deck.

'Do you know Find the Lady?' he says. 'You've just got to pick the Queen of hearts. I show you the cards and then throw them down. And you put a finger on the back of the right one.'

'OK. I'll have a go.'

Danny shows the cards, then flops the cards down, overthrowing the queen in a beautifully disguised sleight. Would fool anyone.

'That one!' Sing Sing says. And she's right.

'Again,' she says. 'Double or quits . . .'

In three goes, she finds the Queen twice. That's unheard of – normally he can confuse even the seasoned circus folk who know the scam backwards. A bit annoying to be outdone, he thinks. But it just adds to the intrigue that clings to Sing Sing like an exotic fragrance.

'Very good,' she says. 'But I grew up around stuff like that. And sometimes it's hard to hide the lady, isn't it? So maybe we find your aunt!'

'With you two on the case, anything's possible,' Zamora says. 'So what happens when we get to Cheung Chau?'

'Find the pier that Lo scribbled on the Post-it note,' Danny says. 'And then improvise.'

The ferry engines ease down as they rumble through the solid arms of Cheung Chau's typhoon walls into a picture-postcard harbour.

A few windsurfers are visible in the distance, their white sails carefree and unencumbered as they run with the wind and the last of the light.

The harbour itself is crammed with fishing boats. They bob against the quayside, some offloading their catch, some readying for sea or awaiting their crews, some abandoned and forgotten and burning slowly with rust. Along the quayside coloured lights are winking into life, making the fish stalls and bars and restaurants look festive. A holiday atmosphere – its tranquillity deepened by the complete absence of cars on the island's little roads.

'OK, boys,' Sing Sing says as the ferry disgorges its

232

passengers and they shuffle down the ramp. 'I'll go and ask about Sai Wan Pier. You keep your eyes open.'

Danny watches her go, then scans the surroundings, his eyes sparking green and brown. The harbourside is a world away from the one they have left just half an hour ago. Small buildings cluster the quayside sprouting sun-bleached awnings and washing flapping in the breeze. To either side of the village, the houses run away on the undulating spine of the landscape, slowly giving way to low peaceful hills, like sleeping dogs in the warm evening. Small groups of tourists relax in the bars, but they're outnumbered by locals taking the air. A constant shuffle of bikes, the ringing of their bells. In any other circumstances this would be a place to switch off and unwind. But now Danny's pulse is kicking quick time. Will there be Triads alerted to watch for them even here? Or is the real danger still to come when they find Sai Wan?

Sing Sing trots quickly back towards them.

'OK. The pier's just round the other end of this bay, past the Thousand Buddha Temple.'

'The what?' Zamora says.

'Tourist trap these days,' she says. 'But very beautiful. We can take a trishaw.'

'Did you ask if anyone had seen Aunt Laura?'

233

Danny says as they head for a tangle of waiting pedal cabs.

'No. We need to keep a low profile,' she murmurs. 'Lots of Triad on this anthill.'

She and Danny hop into the trishaw on the stand and Zamora takes the next.

'Sai Wan Pier, please,' Sing Sing says. 'And get a move on!'

Their rider pushes down his strong, sinewy legs on the pedals and they're away along the quayside, for all the world as if they're just off to take the evening air too.

At one of the rowdier bars, a middle-aged man with cropped bleached hair sits slumped in his plastic chair, mobile held hard to his ear. He puts his little finger in the other one to concentrate over the noise. Getting hurriedly to his feet, he scowls and stomps out into the road.

In the distance Zamora's bowler is just visible over the seat of the second trishaw.

The man hangs up abruptly, then punches another number on his phone, walking down the street, talking fast all the while. From a small gap between the shops and houses a mini police car emerges. The driver beckons to the man with bleached hair and sets his blue flashers spinning.

9 HOW TO BE PERFECTLY STILL AMIDST CHAOS

In the front trishaw Sing Sing turns to Danny. 'Guy in the bar told me there are occasional boat trips from that pier. Fishing business. And some tourist stuff to outer islands. Wanshans.'

'The what Shans?'

'Hundred or more little islands. Some have maybe twenty, thirty people on them. Others deserted.'

'We should get a message to Ricard, shouldn't we?'

Sing Sing scrunches up her face, shaking her head. 'Only if he answers the phone. If we leave a voicemail there's no telling who may get it. And his home line may be tapped. That *gwai daan* Lo's out to get him. Trying to frame him up.'

'*Gwai daan?*'

'Turtle egg. Idiot.'

They're passing a row of fish stalls – every shape and hue of sea creature Danny has ever imagined, all hauled from the depths, some still alive in plastic tanks, others gasping their last on beds of ice. He stares at them as they whip past. For them it's like drowning . . .

The buildings start to space out as they move away from the heart of Cheung Chau village, and they run on into the evening, clinging to the shoreline. A breeze slides in off the South China Sea. Sing Sing taps Danny's shoulder and points out to where it has come from, into the vast emptiness beyond.

'Typhoon season,' she says. 'Think there might be something brewing out there . . .'

Her voice trails off.

Two men are standing in the middle of the street. They've got a small cart – a kind of souped-up golf buggy – turned across the trishaws' path, blocking the route. It sits on big, all-terrain tyres, and its striped canopy flaps in the wind. The men are waving to the lead cyclist to stop, their faces dark. They're not out to play golf, that's for sure, Danny thinks, gripping his set that little bit tighter.

'Triads,' Sing Sing says, as their driver brakes hard and looks around at his passengers uncertainly.

Zamora's cab pulls level.

'Trouble?' he says, getting to his feet like a sea captain on his bridge, peering forward. Sing Sing nods.

'Local boys, I think. After the reward. I'll see if I can talk them round. Uncle Charlie's name can still scare the pants off some of them. Stay here.'

'Come off it, Miss Sing, I can't let you—'

'No arguing!'

She jumps down from the trishaw and marches briskly towards the two men. Again the staccato Cantonese, waving her hands, as if *they* are the ones who should be scared of *her*.

'She's a real live wire, that one,' Zamora says. 'Perhaps I should give her a hand though.'

'Wait a minute, Major. She knows what she's doing.'

Sing Sing is pushing one of the men repeatedly in the chest, her voice crisp on the evening air. She's trying to take the momentum, Danny realizes. Put them on the back foot. But the man's smile is brittle on his flattened face, about to snap. Might need a plan B.

Danny looks around, assessing their situation. Above and to the left of the buggy and the heated conversation squats a temple. Stylized lions stand guard, weathered and smoothed by the sea winds, and writhing dragons spiral along the length of its ornate roof. Beneath that, vermilion pillars shield a darkened space beyond. The bite of incense on the breeze.

No obvious way out, a high wall either side of the temple. Sea to the other side . . .

An engine is approaching from behind them. Danny glances around to see a low-slung Harley Davidson motorbike rumbling to a stop beside his cab. The rider, an elderly man in an oversized biker's jacket, peers at them quizzically, and then gets off to see what the hold-up is. He spits a chunk of phlegm into the dust and then stomps away to the cart blocking the road, his own voice raised in the argument.

The Triads look up, distracted.

Suddenly Sing Sing takes her chance. She snaps into action, kicking out hard at one of the two men, winding him badly – but before she can react the other has her by the shoulders. She tries to throw him, but he's ready for her and sweeps hard with his foot, throwing her off balance.

'Run, boys! RUN!' she shouts, blocking a crunching blow. The elderly bike rider is shouting angrily now, trying to wade into the brawl to help Sing Sing. He wrestles one of the men to the ground, but is then whacked over the back of the head and slumps unconscious into the gutter. Another gangster kicks him for good measure.

Zamora glances over his shoulder. There's a siren just audible in the distance.

'Let's go, Danny. We'll just borrow that poor man's bike . . .'

'We should help. And we can't leave Sing Sing.'

Zamora is already astride the rumbling Harley. 'No choice, Danny.'

Sing Sing's back on her feet, giving as good as she gets. Rapidly parrying blows from both men, then driving them backwards. She glances back at Danny.

'Move it, Woo!' she shouts. 'It's you they want, not me. Get out of here!'

Danny hesitates as the words hit home. *It's you they want.* Not just these men blocking their way. Maybe not even just the Black Dragon? It's starting to feel like everything's been pointing towards a confrontation – that focuses on him. Is that possible? Ricard and Sing Sing and Chow and Lo all seemed to know something about him, to be somehow expecting to see him. And yet the decision to travel was so last minute. Fired by the explosion at school.

But then there were those dots on the charred paper. This isn't about Laura at all. Not really. It's about me. They're after me. But why? And who are *they*?

'Get on the bike, Danny,' Zamora shouts, revving

the throttle. 'We can't help Laura if we're cooling our heels in some police cell. Or worse.'

Danny takes one more look at Sing Sing. It seems like she's about to break free and make a run for it, and glances their way, her fierce gaze urging him to move. That decides it. He jumps onto the pillion, throwing his arms around the Major's solid form. Two more men have appeared from out of the shadows of the temple, drawing guns from shoulder holsters. Definitely not monks . . .

'I can just reach the shifter,' Zamora says. 'Here we go!'

And they're away, engine packing high and hard as the dwarf twists the throttle open.

'Just like the old days!'

Except now they're not riding horizontally around the caged walls of a fairground thrill – but hurtling towards thugs with guns who want to stop them dead in their tracks.

'Showtime,' Zamora shouts. Danny grips for all he's worth as the acceleration throws him back on the Harley's seat. The dwarf flicks the bike left, deliberately veering towards the corner of a boat ramp. They strike it with a bone-jarring jolt – and then they're airborne. It feels effortless. The wind rushing through Danny's hair, whooshing in his ears, the bike's engine revving high. He glances to the left, and there – for the briefest of moments, but in perfect detail – sees a huge golden Buddha spotlit in the deep recesses of the temple. Time stops. Eyes half closed, the Buddha sits in the lotus position, one hand reaching out to touch the altar on which he sits. The image is gone in a second, but it sears itself onto Danny's retina. Perfect stillness against the fury of their escape. He closes his eyes and tucks his head behind Zamora's back – the after-image of the golden figure still glowing in his vision. Gunshots crackle around them – and Zamora lets loose his old war whoop, the one that he used to enter the Wall of Death ride.

The Triad men duck as the motorbike carves the air in a perfect arc. Its back wheel clips the buggy's bonnet and then – with a wobble – Zamora's landed it and is forcing it away down the seafront road.

'Bit rusty,' he shouts. 'But you can't really forget these things.'

Glancing over his shoulder Danny can see three men jumping into their cart, gunning the thing into life. Heading their way. The police lights flashing behind.

But where's Sing Sing? She seems to have vanished

into thin air. Maybe the Buddha will look out for her.

The sense of serenity still holds him, even as two more gunshots ring out across the growl of their Harley.

10 HOW TO IMPROVISE ON A BORROWED BIKE

One of Danny's earliest memories is of leaning over the railing of the Wall of Death watching a younger Zamora fly around its vertical caged walls. The white crash helmet with its big red Z drawing circles in the gloom as the Major practised deep into the evening. It all came to an end one evening with a front-wheel blowout that sent Zamora flying and left him in traction for weeks. He never got on the bike again in earnest after that, other than to potter round the encampment. And it's been almost eight years since. Just have to trust that these things stick in the body memory, Danny thinks.

He throws another quick look over his shoulder, hoping for a glimpse of Sing Sing. Wouldn't put it past her to see her slim form silhouetted and crouched on the temple roof. But there's not a sign.

And instead he sees the buggy closing the gap on

them. Its angry snarl audible over the motorbike's rumble, the men on board it bent low and hanging on for dear life as it bounds along in pursuit.

Danny taps Zamora on the shoulder.

'Company.'

'So, they want a chase? Well, we can easily outrun them on this baby. Oh boy!'

The Major accelerates along the bay road. His wing mirror shows the two round eyes of the buggy falling further behind.

'Told you.'

But it's hard to keep up the speed. The narrow road is cluttered with pedestrians, bicycles, other trishaws and Zamora has to brake and weave. A café has run its tables out almost completely across the path and he has to slow right down to negotiate the obstacle.

'Sorry! Coming through.' He accelerates again.

The buggy is closing fast again; it shows much less concern for the customers in the café. Horn blaring, it mounts the tiny pavement, clips a plastic chair and sends it cartwheeling onto the beach.

'All under control,' Zamora bellows. 'We'll lose them on a clear straight.'

But then, looking up, they see the road ahead is well and truly blocked again. A line of four more tough-looking gangsters, stand across the road, weapons drawn. Red and white roadwork barriers have been dragged across the road, and a mini-digger parked sideways beyond that. One of the men is holding up both his hands, ordering them to stop.

Can't turn around, can't go on, Danny thinks. They'll shoot first, ask questions later. If they bother to ask questions at all. So – give ourselves up? And then what? Let Laura suffer on her own? Or will we be rotting in some cell with her?

Zamora's looking left and right. On the landward side of the path is a wide, spiralling staircase leading up between the houses. Its concrete wall is pocked and chipped, white railings curling away into the gloom – but the angle might be just right. And riding the surface of the wall should be much faster than the stairs and the risk of blowout. Probably safer really. Definitely better than trying to run the roadblock.

'*No hay problema*, Mister Danny,' Zamora barks, as much to reassure himself as Danny. One man at the roadblock has drawn a pistol and is advancing towards them, levelling it at them.

Zamora screws his eyes tight, wringing every ounce of speed from the Harley. He just needs to reach the spiral walkway first. It's a matter of hitting the dropped kerb at just the right angle to hop the bike up over the first step. And then hope for the best. Hope for the magic to come flooding back!

The buggy is zipping up the gap behind them. Danny can almost feel the bead that the passengers are taking on his back with their guns. He looks ahead and spots the curving stairway, feels the bike shearing towards it. Surely not! No way . . .

'Come on, Major Zee!' Zamora mutters to himself, and they slam against the kerb.

A perfect angle. The motorbike pops into the air and Zamora throws his weight simultaneously to the right, unbalancing them, sending them flying almost horizontally. Danny braces for the smash of the impact . . .

But then the wheels have found the curving concrete wall, and Zamora's accelerating as hard as he can, and they're still moving, the bike cutting a tight arc, miraculously climbing the looping retainer wall of the stone steps, wheels skittering for purchase – but keeping grip. It's years since he's cut a line like this, but his hands and arms and legs remember the drill.

'Hot Dog!' he shouts. *'Perfecto!'*

Danny's grinning now, in spite of everything, trying to keep his eyes open, feeling the g force push against the wall. It's all over in a moment, the bike levelling out as Zamora brings them off the wall, onto the path above. Danny lets loose his own whoop of exhilaration. More relief than anything. And the dwarf punches the air like he always did when the hardest trick of the night was done.

Below them the buggy has come to a juddering halt, riders craning their necks to watch Zamora and Danny hurtle up in a curve and disappear from sight between the trees.

The driver grabs a helmet and straps it on, and – taking a quick glance at his chunky tyres – does a three-point turn. Two more of the Triad men pile on board under the jaunty canopy and then the cart's away, bumping powerfully up the stairway in pursuit.

Zamora and Danny thunder along an alleyway, the evening gathering around them. There's washing strung over their heads. People are watering their plants or sitting on doorsteps in the cool. Birds sing from their cages. Dogs curl on front steps. All look up as dwarf and boy race past, shattering the calm.

Zamora flicks on the headlight.

'Make way for a daredevil!'

'Where are we heading?' shouts Danny.

'I think we're still improvising.'

The alleyway twists left, then right, then suddenly drops six steps before Zamora's seen it. But it's no problem. He steadies the bike in mid-flight and lands them with a skid that's just about under control. They come to a stop at a tiny crossroads, engine idling.

'All coming back to me now. Which way, Mister Danny?'

'Left'll take us back to the harbour road. We should still try and head for the pier.'

But now the engine of the chasing buggy is echoing down the alleyway.

'Let's lose this josser first,' Zamora says. He swings the Harley right, into an even tighter alley that cuts sharply up the hillside, left foot rapidly kicking up the gears. The buggy comes into view behind them, its helmeted driver gripping the wheel as it comes bouncing down the stairs, the other Triads clinging to their seats and trying to take aim at the same time.

The front passenger just manages to squeeze off a round and a pot plant on a balcony just over Danny's head explodes, fine soil and petals raining down.

Zamora weaves up the narrowing switchback path. Occasional gaps show between the buildings, the harbour spread out below with its twinkling lights.

Dodging round a corner, they miss by a fraction a man pushing a heavily laden bicycle. His mouth opens as they flash past, shouting a warning. But it's too late. Zamora can do nothing to avoid the elderly men clustered around their Mah Jong game in the middle of the path. The tiles are spread on a couple of beer crates and Zamora hits them hard, sending the players tumbling from their chairs, the pieces clattering through the air like shrapnel.

The angry shouts of the Mah Jong players cut against the revving engine of the pursuing buggy.

They're gaining.

'Faster, Major.'

'Doing my best.'

The path bursts clear of the houses, tarmac giving way to dirt, climbing up into the trees. Bark and earth spit out from the wheels, as they surge on up the hill.

'We'll lose them in the trees . . .'

There's another couple of gunshots and the bike judders. A hit?

But no, nothing hurts and Major Zee looks fine. Danny cranes around again on the pillion and sees the front passenger aiming his gun, standing up and clinging on to the canopy with the other hand. A sudden stink of petrol floods Danny's nostrils.

'Losing power,' Zamora shouts. 'Fuel line's ruptured. Or the tank.'

The Harley is slowing, sputtering. Dying beneath them.

A vague path breaks away to their right, diving away through the trees.

'We'll use gravity,' Zamora shouts, and with the last gasp of the engine, flicks the bike back down the hillside.

Dodging between tree trunks and dense undergrowth, the Harley drops fast, suspension chattering on the rough ground, shaking Danny so hard that it feels like his teeth will come loose at the roots. The track, indistinct to start with, is petering out.

'Not . . . sure . . . about this . . .' the Major is saying, and then suddenly the ground is gone from under them, has become almost vertical, and they are freefalling chaotically, spinning, riders and machine parting company, branches and leaves whiplashing their faces. Danny is crashing from one bush to the next in a confusion of foliage. A scratch sears across his face, another tears his forearm – and he lands on his back, winded, in a stinking pile of leaves and weeds.

The bike clatters on a bit further, rights itself, and

then – like a mortally wounded animal – falls to its side, front wheel still turning, trying to get traction on the air.

Its hot metal ticks in the sudden silence.

11 HOW TO REACH THE END OF THE ROAD

Danny looks around. He can smell the crushed leaves and rotting vegetation mingling with the stinking trail of petrol. Where's Zamora? Gingerly he gets to his feet.

There's the sound of an engine close by. He freezes – but no. It's not the buggy. Something else. More suburban – like a lawnmower.

They've fallen into some kind of large garden, and a path runs away through deep pools of shadow, between flowerbeds and bushes, back in the direction of the village.

'Major?' Danny's voice sounds thin and alone.

'MAJOR?'

There's a rustling in the bush above him as the Major wriggles free of a massive rhododendron and comes sprawling down the slope, head first. Not a very dignified landing, but no worse than many in the circus.

Zamora looks up quizzically. 'Compost heap. You OK?'

'Yes. I think so.'

'Suppose you haven't seen my blinking bowler, have you? Lost it for good now.'

The engine is still rattling away close by. Zamora cocks his head.

'That's not anything that was chasing us. Let's take a look.'

They trot along the side of the path, keeping tight under the smudged shadows of the bushes. Around the corner they see a gardener wafting a leaf blower across the lawn, his back turned on a quad bike and trailer.

'Second theft of the day,' Zamora says. 'But we need to get a damn move on!'

The gardener is wearing ear defenders against the whine of the leaf blower and with his back turned has no idea of what is happening behind him. Danny and Zamora sprint across the grass and onto the quad bike. Zamora turns the key, kicks the thing into life and they're powering down the driveway. Behind them the leaf-filled trailer bangs away, chucking up its contents as they round a corner. Double iron gates stand wide open and they're out into a narrow backstreet.

But their luck is running out and their timing bad.

The buggy driver is idling back down the same lane, his passengers scouring the surroundings for the crash site of the Harley. They all see Danny and Zamora at the same moment – and the driver accelerates hard, piling on the speed. A volley of shots barks out above the noise of the engines.

They'll be on us in seconds, Danny thinks. No time to warm Zamora. He looks down at the coupling to the trailer.

Might be slowing us down. If I can just work it loose . . .

He eases back off the quad bike seat, and, keeping tight hold of the Major's jacket with one hand, reaches down towards the ball and socket towing point. It's like a mini version of the coupling on the circus trailer. You just squeeze and lift the handle and—

It's gone. The quad bike leaps forward down the hill, with Danny desperately clinging on, trying to regain his seat. The trailer's chaotic path catches their chasers off guard. It bangs against a wall, upsets a crate of watermelons tucked beside the path, and then flips over right in front of the buggy. Machine and passengers go flying head over heels, through the rolling watermelons, slamming into a stack of plastic crates. Looking back, Danny just has time to see the chaos: pulped green watermelon, fishing nets and traps, starfish cascading in the streetlight . . .

Then an almighty crunch as metal and bone and jaunty canopy slam into the wall. It sounds bad.

A few minutes later, following the flow of the land back down to the sea, they find themselves emerging onto the bay road near the spiralling stone steps. Not a trace of any of the Triads.

And no sign of Sing Sing.

'Another lap?' Zamora says, looking grim. 'Or shall we get moving?'

'The pier's all we've got. If Sing Sing got free she'll head there,' Danny says. 'And if they got her then we've no idea where she is. Let's keep going.'

They head south again, following the bay road as it twists and turns through a darker, more ragged part of the bay. The sea surges below them, white surf thrumming on the rocks.

A few hundred metres further on a tourist sign gives directions in both Chinese and English.

CHEUNG PO TSAI CAVE. 1.5 KM

SAI WAN PIER. 2 KM

The trail leads them around the curve of the bay, past holiday chalets, thicker trees and undergrowth. And then they glimpse a long finger of concrete stretching out into the waves of the bay, a dark line on the water. It looks deserted.

A few more bends and they have arrived.

There are no boats tied up against the pier – and not much else to see. Just a few bollards, a lifebelt, some steps at the far end for embarking and disembarking. The waves sigh against the rocky beach. No other sound but the high-pitched ringing of a set of windbells hanging from the gutter of a long, low concrete shed.

If this is it – their destination, the big hope from all the clues – then it's a big anti-climax. Not quite the moment of destiny that Danny has been anticipating. No confrontation with the Dragon. No sign of Laura struggling to free herself. Just an empty, stained concrete pier and the sea beyond.

He turns his attention to the shed – it seems there are actually three of them, rammed together back to back. Every window is dark. Nothing is parked out front and no sign of life. Weeds and wildflowers force through the cracked roadway.

Danny gets off the quad bike and walks over, eyes

piercing the gathering gloom.

'Laura?'

The windbells shake in the strengthening wind.

'Sing Sing?'

No reply.

A sign is tacked to the door on the first of the sheds. In rough lettering under a string of Chinese characters: CHARTER BOAT TO WANSHAN. AND OTHERS.

And then, below it, chalked at ankle height, is that same dotted pattern once again. The forty-nine dots. Small, but neatly and deliberately done. Same one circled as on Pony Tail's tattoo.

Danny feels his stomach tightening, palms sweating. His mouth is dry.

'Come on, Major. We must be getting warmer. Even if there's no one here now.'

'Want me to smash the lock?'

Danny nods. There's no time to spare, he thinks. And my hands are shaking. Wouldn't do so well with the picks now.

He looks out at the empty pier, the wide, dark sea beyond, and wonders if they have – after all – reached the end of the trail.

Whether they are too late.

12 HOW TO COAX A BEAM IN THE DARKNESS

Zamora picks up a heavy boulder and brings it down sharply on the padlock, sending echoes racing away across the water. He nods to Danny and they push through the door.

It's dark and silent in the first of the sheds. A smell of dead fish, mould, damp wood choking the air. Just enough light spilling through the doorway to show a desk, a lamp, some mismatching office furniture. Thick gloom beyond that.

'Hello?' His voice is swallowed, silenced by the thickening atmosphere.

Danny clicks on the anglepoise lamp on the desk. It shows a slew of papers covered with scribbled Chinese characters, a couple of nautical charts. He moves them around, squinting for meaning amongst the indecipherable glyphs. On one sheet there's a string of what look like times. Twenty-four-hour clock. Tide tables, Danny wonders. Or sailing times?

There's an apple core half chewed amongst the clutter, browning in the fetid air.

'Someone was here earlier today. Not long ago,' he says, shuffling on down through the papers, fingers working as quickly as they can. Must be something more there to show that their journey has not been a wild chase to nothing. A new clue to follow—

His hands go still as soon as he sees the image, and he takes in a sharp breath. He grabs the crackling sheet of fax paper and holds it to the light. On it – grainy but reproduced clearly enough – is a very familiar face: his own. It's the school photo from Ballstone. The one they took in the first week when he felt all at sea. His startled eyes popped wide in the photographer's flashlight. The mouth forcing a smile, but the whole face clouded with anxiety. Easy to read, he thinks. God, I look as though I'm frozen with fear. His hand is shaking less now, but still it sets the thermal paper whispering in the silence.

'Come and look at this, Major.'

Zamora has been keeping watch by the half-open door. He swears when he sees the photo.

'They've got a picture of *me*!' Danny says. But it's no surprise now. Just confirmation of the chain of events steadily winding around him, snaring him tighter and tighter. Everything and everyone pulling him in towards this moment.

'What do they want with *me*!' It's more indignation than enquiry. He slaps the fax back on the desk.

The dwarf furrows his brow.

'Let's not rush to conclusions, *no*?'

Danny looks back at Zamora.

'It's me they're after,' he says calmly. 'You guessed as much, didn't you? Some time ago? I knew there was something you weren't telling me.'

'Mister Danny. It was only a feeling. And I didn't want to scare you.'

'I'm not a little kid any more.'

'*Claro!* I know that, my friend.' The dwarf pats him on the back. 'I know that.'

'Let's search every inch of this place. And then get out of here.'

At the back of the room a door stands agape. A black rectangle leading into deeper darkness beyond.

There's a torch hanging from a nail on the wall, a big chart pinned to the flaking plasterboard, wreathed in shadow. Danny flicks the torch switch and, in its hesitant yellow beam, picks across the now familiar shapes. There's Kowloon, Hong Kong Island and the Peak, Cheung Chau. From this end of the island, presumably from the pier outside, red lines snake away across the South China Sea.

He follows a couple. They run out past Lantau and Lamma to other islands not far from Hong Kong.

Another track loops away into the emptier quarters of the map. Danny traces it with the torch as it curls towards a cluster of islands much further out into the blankness of the sea. When it reaches the Wanshan Archipelago it starts zipping from one little island to another.

A black cross has been pencilled against a couple of islands that stand apart from the rest. There's no charter service joining them to the others.

'X marks the spot?' Zamora says. 'There's no sign of Miss Laura here. Maybe that's where we have to look.'

Danny nods, then peers into the second doorway. 'Let's check the rest of the sheds, and then get back and find Ricard. Tell him what we've got.'

'And try and find Miss Sing Sing too.'

The torch flickers uncertainly. Danny bangs the end of it on the doorframe, coaxing a bit more juice from the faltering batteries. In its feeble beam the second room gives up a jumble of fishing nets, buoys, chairs, plastic crates, all covered with a thick rime of dust and mildew. The air is heavier still.

There's a path cleared through the junk, and on the objects lying close to it, you can see where fingers and hands have brushed against the grime. Danny lights the pathway with the torch. Two long, jagged trails scuffed on the ground. Parallel lines as if something's been dragged in – or out. Zamora nods.

Halfway across the room there's a hand lying on the floor. A dull blood red. For a moment Danny thinks all his worst fears have been realized – but coming closer he sees it's just a rubber work glove, deflated and forgotten.

Holding my breath, Danny thinks. Need to breathe. Next shed either gives us Laura, or the Dragon . . . or failure. But if Laura's there, surely she would have called out? That's if she *can* call out.

The door at the back of the second room is shut fast. Three heavy bolts are slid across it on their side – the whole thing reinforced with metal shuttering. A cell. They listen at the door, but hear nothing save the blood chugging in their ears, the sea's steady voice outside. A tiny window shows nothing but their own reflections and when Danny tries to shine the torch through it, the faltering glow just bounces back off dirty glass.

They slide back the bolts – greased and smooth in their channels – and push the door open, the hair riffling up on the back of Danny's neck. It's all coming down to this door, this moment. So let's confront it.

The air inside smells worse yet – something he can't place, but which arouses a kind of animal instinct deep down, to be cautious, to keep clear. But, on top of that, there's a telltale note, which Danny recognizes as soon as it hits his nose.

Laura's perfume.

He's never been so glad to smell it. It's as if she's standing there, just out of the torch's reach . . . He almost expects to hear her voice call out to him.

'Laura?' He flicks the beam around in a circle.

But the torch just shows bare walls, an empty room with a barred window that leads onto the blackened hillside behind.

'She was here, Major,' Danny says, excitement and disappointment mixing in his voice. 'She *was* here.'

He scans the wall for any sign of a message or further clues. Laura would let me know, she'd leave me a sign like before . . .

But there's nothing.

The torch stutters out and he bangs it again frantically, and – as he does so – it gives one last burst of light, shining on the bare concrete floor.

And there in its beam is the body of Charlie Chow.

He's lying in the dust, arms and legs bound with wire, head turned at an unnatural angle. Congealing blood soaks his shirt and there's a horrible mess of a gunshot wound to the side of his skull. His eyes are open in surprise, but glazed and empty. He can see nothing now.

'Major!' Danny gasps, his knees sagging under him. 'Major!'

A noise behind him, a kind of snuffled sigh. He spins round, flailing the light to see what's there. But then the battery dies and the beam gutters out, darkness enfolding him.

A shadow flits through the door. Someone behind him.

'Major?'

No. There, to the right.

'Major . . . ?'

And then his head feels very wrong.

There's no pain, just a heaviness – and it feels like he's falling again: in the laundry chute, down the hillside, somewhere far away.

I've messed up, he thinks. Got it all wrong at the vital moment and let everyone down again. Maybe I should ask Dad. No, that's wrong. My fault . . .

He hears Sing Sing's voice in his head. 'Used to call it Death Island.' And then, 'Pleased to meet you, Danny Wooooooo . . .'

He gropes for understanding – his mind trying to summon images, thoughts, struggling to keep consciousness. But it's all muddling together: he sees the golden Buddha serene in his darkened temple, skyscrapers and trams and battered taxis, tumbling cards, the blitz of the firecrackers on the stairs, multi-hued fish – now in an aquarium, now swimming around his father's head in the water torture cell.

He sees white sheets falling like distressed ghosts, then a keyboard, each key bearing the seven by seven dotted pattern, and the dots merge into squiggles and shapes inked on the pages of his father's secret notebook, which turn into flapping crows. And then there are Mum and Dad moving towards each other on the highwire across the deep blue of the Mysterium hemisphere, and the snow is falling heavily from the its ceiling, drifting thickly across his vision and . . .

. . . and that red fish on the restaurant floor, and the lipstick gouge, and the red glove bleeding on the shed floor . . .

. . . and he's on the floor of a deserted shed on a small island thousands of miles from home and everything has gone utterly . . .

. . . BLACK.

ACT THREE

The easiest way to attract a crowd is to let it be known that at a given time, and given place, some one is going to attempt something that in the event of failure will mean sudden death.

Harry Houdini

1 HOW TO PUT YOUR CARDS ON THE TABLE

Pugga pugga pugga . . .

An engine is rocking Danny slowly awake.

This one is solid, steady, in no rush. It fills his ears, slowly drowning the sounds of his fathomless sleep.

His head feels heavy and it throbs in time with the engine.

But he's not quite ready to surface yet. His memory is spooling, looping . . .

. . . pulling him back to that last week in the Mysterium. There was already a tumble of emotions pulling at him then. Things he tried to forget. A bad atmosphere around the encampment all that week. The cold weather blowing in and tightening muscles, hardening faces against the wind and snow. Mum and Dad arguing again, sharply, on the trailer steps, for all to hear.

Mum snapping, 'It's going to catch up with you, Harry.'

And Dad, his voice ragged, 'Lily. We all have our pasts to deal with, dammit! You should know that!'

And she slammed the door on him.

When he had nagged Dad again about having a look through the *Escape Book* he had picked the wrong moment and got told so in no uncertain terms. Very unusual in itself – and it sent him to bed upset, confused, a sense of injustice nagging away. A feeling that the world was out of balance, and that they were poised above a great drop.

Later, he saw the two of them sitting at the big table, silhouetted against the brightly lit big top, holding hands quietly. Reconnecting, repairing. The bulbs over the entrance to the tent still pulsing out *WONDER CHAMBER* into the lengthening night.

That was good. But why would nobody tell him what the trouble was? It was as if he was incidental to the story developing around him – whatever that story was – and surely he was a part of it, even if no one would explain what was going on.

The next night Danny put his plan into action. In the dead hours, long after midnight, he dressed quickly, grabbed his pocket torch, sprang the *Escape Book* from its hidden recess in the cupboard, and stole out into the night.

On the far side of the encampment was the prop store. Always a favourite hideaway for Danny, sitting up amidst the stacked flight cases and trunks, making a comfortable den from the crashmats, surrounded by walking globes, silks and coiled ropes, cyr wheels and the rest of the Mysterium's paraphernalia. Blanco's scruffy dog, Herzog, would often come and find him there and snuggle next to him, snoring rhythmically, reassuring him. The hum of the generators nearby masking any other sounds.

But that night it was hard to get comfortable in the cold. And no sign of Herzog to keep him company. He was trying to keep warm and focus on the pages of code near the back of the *Escape Book* – hoping to gain some kind of enlightenment but unable to make head or tail of the squiggles there – when Rosa came bowling in, switching on the light, startling him.

She raised her eyebrows in two peaked arches, just like she always did when introducing the next act of the *Wonder Chamber* show.

'*Ciao*, Danny. What are you doing here?'

'Just having a rest.'

'Does your papa know where you are?' She turned

and hurriedly put whatever it was she was carrying to the back of the store, out of sight.

'Yes.'

'I bet.' She looked him in the eye. 'Tell you what – I've got some *ribollita* stew on the stove. How about some to warm you up, *bello*? Then I'll take you back over to Harry and Lily.' An offer too good to refuse – he was addicted to Rosa's Italian home cooking and followed her back to her trailer, watching the tattooed roses on her calves peeping over her boot-tops, incongruous against the snow.

He was halfway through the warming, satisfying soup, ladling up beans and carrot, when the alarm was raised.

Fire! Fire!

They both jumped from Rosa's trailer, feet crunching the frozen ground, racing towards the flames curling upwards in ragged question marks, discharging into the sky. Herzog came bounding over, barking furiously. And some of the Klowns following him. And Blanco too. And then Zamora and more of the company – until all of them were gathered together, staring in horror.

The trailer burned fiercely. Fresh snow falling through the long February night, the flakes sizzling, evaporating.

And eventually firehoses dousing the pillar of flame.
But too late.
He was too late . . .

Danny swims up to consciousness – to brightness –
from out of the depths.

Figures blur in his eyes. The engine chugging
away . . .

He blinks hard and takes a deep breath, realizing
that he is alive, that the flurry of images that came
with the blow to the head wasn't his life flashing before
his eyes . . .

Where am I? Not the Mysterium. That was all
memory. Dimly, he's aware that what he's just recalled
is the most sustained burst of memory about the night
of the fire he's ever had. Things are loosening in his
mind.

'Danny? Mister Danny?' Zamora is bending over
him. His powerful short figure rising and falling, rising
and falling.

A quick burst of Cantonese cuts across the engine,
the slap of waves.

'Back off,' Zamora snaps. 'I just want to see if he's
OK, dammit. Make sure you haven't done any
permanent damage, knuckle head.'

'I'm OK,' Danny says slowly. He sits up, looking around, letting his focus sharpen.

They're in a small fishing boat, under a dirty brown awning, the sea surrounding them on every side, brimful of light, dazzling.

The ever present stench of fish comes from a tangle of nets near them. Zamora is sitting next to him, his wrists bound with metres of gaffer tape, his face expectant, eyes bright with emotion.

Danny looks up. Jug Ears sits there, leaning against the side of the boat, keeping Zamora covered with a pistol.

'Old ugly there thumped you with that fist of his,' Zamora says. 'Seems Miss Sing didn't lay him out for long. Dammit, Mister Danny, I'm glad to see you open your eyes.'

'Where are we?'

'All at sea. No idea.'

'How long have we been going?'

'Hours and hours. And we were hours in that stinking shed before that. Couple of old friends with us.'

'Shut your mouth!' Jug Ears gets up, levelling the pistol at Zamora's head.

'You shut yours,' Zamora says. 'If you were going to

kill us you'd have done it by now.' He turns to Danny again. 'Old ugly chops and his pals crept up on us, Danny. At the warehouse. I'm sorry. I was trying to keep watch.'

'That was Chow, wasn't it? The body in the shed, I mean.'

'Yes. Sorry to say it was. But they obviously want us alive – for some reason.'

That fires Danny's heart. A flicker of strength kindling again. So the Sai Wan Pier wasn't the moment of destiny after all. Just another step along the way. But it's coming now, for sure. Boy, he thinks, does my head hurt though. He goes to reach up to feel it and realizes that his hands are bound too. He glares at Jug Ears.

'Where's Sing Sing?'

The man ignores him, just rolls the lollipop along between his teeth.

'Where's my aunt? Where are we going?'

No answer but a shrug of the muscular shoulders.

Danny assesses the situation. There are other men sitting on the deck forward. Pony Tail amongst them. All have pistols tucked in their belts. No idea where they are even if – somehow – they manage to free themselves and overpower their captors. Pony Tail catches his eye for a moment, then looks away quickly. Was that a moment of connection of sorts?

'We're in hot mustard, don't you think?' Zamora says, following Danny's gaze.

'Very hot, Major.' But we're not beaten yet, he adds to himself.

The boat rides the waves, trying to lull Danny back into a concussed sleep. He fights it each time. Need to keep clear about where we are, what the situation is . . . He thinks of the Mysterium logo, the fragile butterflies fluttering around the bleached skull. Black eye sockets. He thinks of his own skull on the seabed – Laura's, Zamora's. Sing Sing too maybe? If we keep sharp maybe we can still get through this.

The sun climbs higher, casting strong shadow under the awning, and the engine keeps chugging away, moving them out across the South China Sea at what feels like the pace of an exhausted snail.

He feels thirsty and looks round to see if there's anything to drink.

Zamora is wriggling beside him.

'Can't get enough play in this damn tape to break free.'

'Not sure that's a good strategy anyway, Major.

Maybe they're just adding us to their kidnap plans.'

'*Caramba*,' the Major sighs. 'I'm just not sure that's their game any more.'

'But they're ransoming Laura.'

'Yes, but—'

The dwarf sits back hard against the side of the fishing boat.

'But what?'

'Cards on the table, Mister Danny?'

'Tell me.'

'Well, it's just this blasted business of the explosion at your school. Laura was really upset about it. I mean, really upset. She phoned me that night. The thing is, she wasn't convinced it was a gas leak, Danny. She thinks it was a bomb. That it was aimed at *you*.'

At last the truth is coming out! At last he could place some of the pieces.

'Which is why they had my photo, why the forty-nine dots were there—'

'And why she was so keen to bring you here. Have me ride shotgun. But it hasn't really worked out, has it? Out of the frying pan and all that.'

'What about Ricard? The photo on his desk. This is all coming back to Mum and Dad, isn't it? Not just me. Something they did. Something in their past.'

'To be honest, I don't know for sure.'

'But you think so?'

'Maybe. Your papa had more than one string to his bow, you know. Think about all the time he spent away from the Mysterium . . .'

'What do you mean?'

'Just that there were deep waters there, Danny. Did you not feel that?'

'I don't know. It's hard to tell what's normal, isn't it? When you're small.' Especially somewhere like the Mysterium.

They're interrupted by the static of a walkie-talkie, a burst of Cantonese. The gang members are all looking out in the same direction across the wide, rolling field of the sea.

Danny scrabbles to his feet, unsteady on the boat's roll. Coming into view are two small islands – furry green caterpillars crawling on the surface of the water.

And anchored tight against one of them is an ugly block of a boat. A bulk carrier, low in the water, figures visible on the deck by the bridge. It's covered with a massive camouflage net, softening its lines, blurring it against the island and the water. But Danny recognizes it at once.

The hijacked cargo ship.

2 HOW TO HANDLE A REUNION IN DIFFICULT CIRCUMSTANCES

It takes another half-hour to get alongside the vessel, but time now feels like it's running very quickly. Soon they are swallowed by the carrier's shadow.

Faces appear over the side and throw down mooring ropes. Then a long rope ladder unfurls, snaking against the boat's side, just long enough to reach. Chips of orange rust falling down on them and the water.

Pony Tail urges Danny and Zamora to their feet.

'You climb now.'

Zamora looks up at the swaying rope ladder, shakes his head. He holds up his hands. 'Can't do it with these taped, now, can we?'

Pony Tail confers with the others in quick whispers. He takes out a razor sharp flick-blade.

'Don't move,' he says to Zamora. 'Don't do stupid thing.'

There's a riffle of safety catches going off as the

thugs surround Danny and Zamora, guns trained on them.

'No problem,' Zamora says. 'I'm incapable of doing anything stupid.'

Pony Tail slices the thick tape around both of their wrists and the circulation goes thickly back into Danny's hands. Pins and needles firing. Agony. But good too. He flexes his fingers, rubs his hands together, massaging life into them.

'Now climb.'

There's no arguing with that firepower, Danny thinks. And I want to see what's going on first. If this *is* about me and Mum and Dad – and not just Laura and the hijack of some rusting bulk carrier – I want to know as much as possible. Even if . . .

Well, don't think about it. Clear the mind. With a blank mind you can't add a judgement – a good or a bad – to the situation. So everything's a lot clearer.

'After you, Mister Danny. Just like climbing to the highwire rig, hey?'

'You'll be fine, Major.' Then he adds as quietly as possible. 'And let's do what they say for now.'

'OK. But if I see a good chance, Danny, by heavens, I'll take it. And as many of them as I can with me!'

It's a good ten metres from the fishing boat to the

deck of the carrier. The rope ladder swings against the hulk of the ship and Zamora shouts, 'Hold the bottom tight, dammit. What kind of roustabouts are you anyway?'

If anything, the twenty or so men on the deck of the hijacked vessel look meaner than any they've yet seen. Unshaven, unwashed, there's a fanatical glow in their eyes. They're all carrying heavier weaponry than Pony Tail and Jug Ears – and train most of it on Danny and Zamora.

In complete silence the gang motion them across the hot deck of the boat. The dappled shadow of the camouflage netting plays across their faces. Nothing else moves.

Danny glances over the side – the smaller of the two islands lies no more than fifty metres away, thickly wooded, surrounded by jagged rocks. The larger island maybe half a kilometre away. Nothing else to be seen but water and sky. Jump and swim for it? Even if you reached the island, what then?

They're marched swiftly to a bulkhead door. There's a steady clicking sound coming from nearby. It takes Danny a moment to find its source – a small box dangling around the neck of a man behind him. A Geiger counter presumably. Keeping check on the radioactive waste in the hold below?

Then they're in a metal-floored companionway and it's much hotter. There's a strong smell of engine oil, cigarette smoke, the pervasive hint of vomit. Down a steep flight of stairs, along another corridor to a watertight door. A sense of claustrophobia starts to tug at Danny's mind.

Turning the round-handled lock, one of the gunmen swings the door open – and he and Zamora are both sent sprawling, tripping over the raised threshold, into the darkened room beyond.

'Danny! Danny!'

A familiar voice calling in relief, alarm. A voice he thought he'd never hear again.

Major Zamora fishes the lighter from his pocket and kindles the flame.

And there in its feeble glow is Laura.

She looks very tired, her face smudged with grime, her hair a strange lopsided mess. She helps Danny up from the floor and hugs him hard.

'I was praying they wouldn't get you. I don't know if I'm glad to see you. Or sad. Bloody hell. My poor boy!'

'*Madre mia*, Miss Laura, it's good to see you though,' Zamora says.

'Are you OK?' Danny asks.

'I'm not sure,' she says. 'It's not been the most wonderful trip, has it? And I've just had the worst haircut ever.'

The door clangs shut behind them and they hear the lock turn.

'I'd like to say I've been in tighter spots than this . . .' Laura says, but lets the thought die. She looks as dejected as Danny has ever seen her look. But he has to ask her now, before it's too late.

'I need to know some things,' he says slowly. 'I need you to tell me about the bomb at school. Anything you know about Dad and haven't told me.'

'OK.' She sits down. 'OK. But first tell me what's been happening. Did you find Ricard? Does he know where we are? If he does, then there's still a chance.'

3 HOW NOT TO JUDGE BY APPEARANCES. AGAIN.

Danny tells their side of the story succinctly, as precisely as he can. No point wasting energy.

'. . . And then we gave the Triads the slip on Cheung Chau. Found the sheds at the pier,' he concludes, rubbing his head. 'We found a chart on the wall. We were about to try and find Sing Sing and go back to Ricard. Then we saw Chow – and then they got us.'

They're sitting in the dark on the bare floor of the storeroom, trying not to move too much, to breathe easily, but the heat and humidity are almost unbearable, pressing against them, sweat welling on their skin.

'God almighty. Poor Charlie,' Laura says. 'He was a decent guy. What about Sing Sing though? Do you think she got away?'

'We don't know.'

Silence.

Laura forces a laugh, trying to lift the atmosphere.

'Well done though, boys! I'd have given anything to see you on that ladder, Major. And the fireworks! And you mesmerizing that Triad, Danny.'

'But we failed,' he says.

'We're not beaten yet. We'll get a chance, I'm sure. Maybe Sing Sing got back to Ricard.'

'So Ricard *is* an *amigo?*' Zamora asks.

'Oh yes. One of the best. I've never met him before, but he comes highly recommended.'

'Who by?' Danny says, but he knows the answer even before Laura says it.

'Your father, Danny. They go waaaay back. We can trust him.'

So my instincts were right, Danny thinks. I read him right. And the link to Dad gives his mood a kickstart.

'And Sing Sing?' he asks. 'And Chow? Where do they fit?'

'Sing Sing kind of works for Ricard now and then. Like an informant – unofficial capacity. Keeping an eye on the nasty fish swimming around Chow. He was generally on the side of the angels since his conversion. But nasty acquaintances. And they never noticed Sing Sing. She's been a part of that world all her life as far as I can tell.'

'And Lo?'

'As bent as you like. Most of the Hong Kong police are clean these days. But he's up to his neck in kickbacks and cover-ups.'

Danny inches closer to Laura.

'And you, Aunt Laura? What happened?'

'Made a mistake. Underestimated the size of their operation. They bundled me into their car and chloroformed me – or something similar. I woke up in that gym or whatever it was and managed to scribble you a message. Then they hooded me, bundled me out the back into another car. Then we had a God-awful drive through the city with me crammed in the boot squashed up against a spare tyre. Then a speedboat to Cheung Chau. Then another one out to here. And I only managed to thump one of them the whole way.'

'But what about Dad? And Ricard? Does this have anything to do—'

The light flickers on overhead, making them all look up – blinking hard – to see the door swinging open, silhouetting a small figure.

'How nice of you all to drop by.'

The figure steps forward into the sickly fluorescent light.

Kwan.

He's squinting through the thick glasses. Smiling at a private joke. Slowly he removes the spectacles and tosses them to one side.

'I forgot to tell you something,' Laura says. 'Guess who's in charge round here.'

Danny stares in disbelief at Mister Kwan. Zamora too.

'*Carajo!* Are you trying to tell me—'

'Yes, Major Zamora. I'm the top dog round here. Mr Kwan, the nice taxi driver. In Chinese we have saying: trying to judge by appearances is like trying to measure the sea with a bucket. Hopeless task.'

'But I picked you randomly! Third one off the rank.'

'Which is what I guessed you would do. Took a bit of doing to elbow into the queue. Time it so that I was in right place at right time. It's quite easy to read what people will do sometimes. But I expect you know about that, Danny. Don't you? A kind of magician's force.'

'Who are you?' Danny says, squaring up to Kwan.

Two gunmen step forward, guns flicked in Danny's face.

'Black Dragon Number One. This is my operation.'

'And what do you want from us? A ransom?'

'Not at all. This ship – the radioactive cargo – that's our bargaining chip. We're selling it on to another party. They want to use it in the Mediterranean. Release the sand onto beaches there, let it blow in the wind. Still radioactive enough to create havoc.' He steps up to Danny. Face to face.

'That's mass murder.'

'That's their business, not ours. I'm just middle man. No, I'm just carrying out orders, Danny. For someone higher up. They want you out of picture. Seems you could cause *big* problems. And they want you dead. It's personal, apparently.'

'No.' Laura's getting to her feet, colour rushing to her face. 'I won't bloody allow it.'

'You don't have a say in it,' Kwan says quietly. 'We're holding all the cards.'

He turns on his heels and is gone, guards backing out, closing the door tight shut.

4 HOW TO STARE DEFEAT IN THE FACE

This time the light is left on. They sit huddled together in the middle of the floor. No windows, just a small ventilation grille high on the wall. Danny hugs his knees and looks from Laura's face to Zamora's and back again. Neither of them can meet his eyes, and both gaze down at the stained floor.

'But . . . what does he mean, "someone higher up"? What am *I* supposed to know?' he says, and this time he can't hide the impatience in his voice. He needs to know. So much is always hidden from him, he feels. Mum, Dad, then Zamora and presumably his guardian too! They all think they know best, that he's just a kid to be protected from the truth. But that's wrong. Wasn't the trailer fire the day he grew up? The return of anger is strong enough to drown out any fear. For now. It flickered briefly into life after the ladder escape.

Long held in check, the emotion forces its way out now.

'Tell me!' he shouts. 'Tell me what's going on! Now!'

Laura shuffles uneasily. 'I'm starting to think this myth of the Forty Nine may not be so much of a myth after all, Danny. I don't know much, to be honest. Always thought they used it to frighten the sheep. Stop people prying into the bigger organized crime gangs. But what with the diagrams, the explosion at your school—'

'And how's Dad involved? Why am *I* involved?'

'Your dad worked for Inspector Ricard from time to time, Danny. They – Interpol – called Harry in when they needed special skills. Hypnotism, "mind reading", impossible bugging or surveillance operations, that kind of thing.'

And although Danny's mouth drops open at this, for some reason he isn't completely surprised. Now he comes to think about it – beyond the card tricks, the warm smile, beyond the Mysterium – beyond the husband and father, was another man, one with eyes on a further horizon.

Zamora shakes his head. 'Well, bless my soul. I thought he was up to something.'

Laura puts her hand on Danny's shoulder. 'He was sworn to secrecy. Not even Lily really knew. Your dad took his confidentiality clause very seriously. And I only know little bits.'

'And how do you know?'

'Harry sent me a letter. Just before he and Lily died. It said that he hoped I would look after you if . . . if anything happened to them. He said that you could "take care of things", Danny. That you had the ability and the heart to do the right thing. That you would find the things you needed close to you. The key, he called it.'

'Why didn't you tell me all this before?'

'I was waiting for you to get a bit bigger . . . and trying to fill in the gaps. See what he had been up against.'

Zamora's nodding now.

'It makes sense. I always knew he was up to more than guest billings at other circuses. Otherwise he'd have taken me, wouldn't he? I even thought he was having an affair at one point. May he forgive me!'

'But why did they want to kill Dad?'

'There I'm guessing. Maybe he'd angered someone very powerful. Maybe he'd found something that was going to expose the Forty Nine. I don't know.'

Danny fingers the lock pick around his neck. He's almost forgotten it was there. Now he holds it tight – a palpable link to his past. Is that 'the key'? It seems too obvious for Dad. He liked to hide things in riddles.

Something else then? Maybe whatever Dad meant him to keep was burned to a cinder in the fire. There were a few things he kept in the strongbox under a bunk.

There was money in there. Passports. Birth certificates. Nothing obvious . . .

But then he knows. It must be the *Escape Book* – it must be! What was the first quote written in there, printed in neat capitals? LIFE IS A NEVER-ENDING MYSTERY, BUT THE KEY IS ALWAYS IN YOUR HANDS. But then how would Dad know that Danny would run away with it that night? How would he know that Danny would keep the thing safe?

He bites hard on his lip. Thinks about the notebook tucked in the secret compartment in his own desk back home. Say nothing. Not for now, anyway. Nice to have my own secret . . . And, if we ever get out of this, that's the first thing I'm going to do. Take another look at Dad's notes and diagrams. Have another go at cracking his codes – if we ever get out of this.

The anger is gone again, its energy mutating back

into concentration. When Laura glances anxiously his way she is astonished to see the look firing his two-coloured eyes: the kind of thing she saw on her rare visits to the Mysterium, playing in Harry's eyes before he attempted a new and potentially dangerous trick. What he called 'A thousand-yard stare'. The determination to face down the danger.

To believe that something seemingly impossible was actually possible.

5 HOW TO PREPARE FOR THE WORST

Another hour drags by. The heat is still intense, stifling the storeroom. It doesn't feel like they've got much oxygen left.

'At least the sun will be down soon,' Laura says. 'Then it might at least start to cool down a bit . . .' Her voice falters. It feels such a lame thing to say. Danny needs more than that from her.

'Did you manage to see much of the ship?' he says. It feels better to be thinking – at least going through the act of planning – than simply waiting. I feel strangely calm, he thinks. Like everything's been building to this. For days, weeks. All my life. I'm going to face it squarely. And if it's the end . . . ?

Then better to go out like that. Calm. Clear headed. Wonder what Mum and Dad thought, felt . . . Did they know it was the end? I'll never know. Danny breathes in sharply.

'Well? Did you see much of the ship, Aunt Laura?' he repeats.

'Not much. We came in darkness. There's the cargo tanks, a service deck up front. Lots of it taped off with radiation warnings. All the crew quarters, engine rooms, stores like this, the bridge, are all here at the stern. Some of the ship's crew are still on board, I think. Prisoners.'

'How many of the Dragon?'

'Twenty-ish? Armed to the teeth. Looks like they're expecting a war.'

'We'll get a chance,' Zamora says, cracking his knuckles one after the other to clear his head. 'Give it a go.' But he doesn't sound convinced.

And then, deep below them, the engines grumble into life without warning. The ship vibrates and rattles as if it will shake itself to pieces. Sounds like every bolt in the hulk is working loose. Then they're moving.

What does it mean? Danny listens hard, trying to pick out any sound that will give him a clue as to what Kwan and the Dragon are doing. But the shudder of the engines lasts no longer than ten or so minutes and then the engines die, and in the silence they hear the distant roar of the anchor chain as it drops to the seabed.

'Moving away from the island, perhaps?' Laura says. 'But why?'

From some way off, they hear the buzz of a much smaller engine now. The waspy sound of a motor launch. You can hear the slap, slap, slap as it skips across the waves. It cuts close. Closer. Comes alongside and falls to an idle.

No one says a word in the cell. No one wants to voice the thought that this might be the police, that this might be rescue . . .

But nothing happens and, as the minutes drag out, their hopes gradually subside.

And then the door opens again. Pony Tail and Jug Ears are back, along with some of the other gunmen. They urge Danny from the cabin, then indicate that Laura and Zamora should follow.

'What's going on?' Laura demands. 'He's just a little kid. What do you want with him? Why make it worse for yourself when the police get here? Which they will. Believe me!'

But the men say nothing.

They look rather solemn – almost embarrassed – and any animosity displayed in the rumble on the Peak

298

has been replaced with something more subdued. Pony Tail keeps his eyes half shut as he pushes Danny in the back. And the grin is gone from Jug Ears' flat face.

'I wish you'd get rid of that abominable shirt,' Zamora says, trying to rile the Triad man. 'It doesn't do anything for you. Oi, you. Ugly – I'm talking to you.' The big man just shakes his head.

Danny's heart is drumming in his ears now. There's no denying the fear. Whatever is coming is close at hand, subduing even these two hardened gangsters into silence. What on earth can it be? Time to try and reach out.

He looks at Pony Tail's back.

'Tony. Tony? I want you to relax and listen to me.'

The man just waves his hand in the air. 'Don't speak.' He glances back then and adds, 'Save your strength.'

They all troop through the network of hot, fetid corridors, back up the companionway. And onto the deck, the fresh air coming as a relief after the hours of confinement below.

Evening is falling across the water, the sun splaying through the oncoming rush of clouds.

'Bad weather, I reckon,' Zamora says, but his eyes

are scanning the men and their guns, waiting for a moment, waiting for the chance to take them down. Danny glances at the distant horizon. He tries to deepen his breathing. One breath at a time. Don't allow the emotion and tension to take you where you don't want to go.

'Move it,' Jug Ears grunts.

They're shunted along the side of the main deck as the boat heaves on the gathering swell. Then up three flights of metal steps onto a broad helicopter pad behind the bridge.

Kwan is waiting for them, tapping a foot impatiently on the deck.

He waits for Danny to be brought to the middle of the large yellow 'H' in its circle and clears his throat. 'Roll up,' he shouts, 'ROLL UP! Ladies and gentlemen. Roll up and see one of the greatest shows on earth!'

Danny looks around him. The last of the sun splinters through the camouflage netting onto the deck. The Black Dragon are arrayed in that glow, waiting, watching. He's the centre of attention clearly in what looks like a horrible parody of the big top.

He checks his breathing again. It's deep and steady now. And that in turn is steadying his pulse, taking it back down to just a shade faster than normal. Nothing like how it can thump when Jamie's got it in for him. Weird. The school grounds seem light years distant. But the world of the Mysterium somehow very close at hand.

'Attention here, please, Mister Woo,' Kwan barks, an irritable note creeping into his voice. 'Now, don't think this is *my* idea. It seems . . . somewhat excessive. We could just shoot you like that double-crosser Chow and send you floating down to the fishes . . . But something more *fitting* has been suggested to me.'

There's a large packing crate standing on end next to Kwan. He snaps his fingers like a showman of old and two of the guards step forward to open it to reveal a tall freezer inside.

'Apparently you will be familiar with a version of this. I'm afraid it's the best we could do given the timescale. We've drilled some holes so that it will sink quickly. It should all be over in a few minutes.'

'No!' Laura gasps, stepping forward. 'That's hideous. You can't do it!'

Three Triad members grab her, pinning her arms tight to her side, holding her head whilst they put tape across her mouth.

'. . . you . . . mmph . . . bas-mphhh . . . fu . . . mphhh . . .'

With attention diverted, Zamora takes his chance. He brings his elbow smartly back into the groin of the closest guard, who howls in pain, crumpling to the floor. The dwarf spins and punches a cracking blow hard up into the jaw of the man beside him.

But a third strikes him hard over the back of the neck, and a fourth has a gun muzzle lodged against his head. He keeps struggling and it takes two more to pin him down to the hot metal of the deck. Kwan watches impassively. When calm is restored he signals to a guard on the door nearby.

'Bring on the volunteer from the audience, please.'

The bulkhead door is opened–and Sing Sing is escorted onto the helipad.

She sees Danny, sees Laura and Zamora, and takes in the whole situation in a second. She rolls her eyes. Scared and exasperated all at once.

'A friend of yours, I believe.'

Danny's mouth opens, but he can't find the words he needs. He's glad to see Sing Sing is alive. Dismayed that she too is captive, whilst simultaneously glad that she is with him now. A real friend. Sing Sing isn't like the others at school. She feels real. As real as life used to feel in the Mysterium. In the old days. And all too late!

'It'll be OK, Danny,' Sing Sing shouts. 'I'm so glad to know you.'

Danny smiles, fighting the emotion.

'Very touching I'm sure,' Kwan says, cutting the air with his hand as if chopping the conversation short. 'Let's get this over with so I can report back.'

Danny's breathing has lost its calm. Must get control back. Must be in the moment. Every bit of attention on the cutting edge of *now*.

Because it's as clear as day what is coming. It'll be a repeat of the water torture cell. He's going to be put to the test that not even Dad could manage.

'Handcuffs for your wrists,' Kwan is saying. 'A few chains for your arms and legs. Padlocks. And then we'll tape the whole thing shut . . . and *baai baai*.'

'No!' Sing Sing snaps. She wrenches free of her captor, runs across the deck to Danny and throws her arms around him.

'Chinese proverb,' she says through a muffled sob. '"Teachers open the door. But you enter by yourself." You can do it.'

She's pulled roughly away, doing her best to kick the shins of anyone within striking distance, eyes firing menace at anyone who will meet them.

'My own volunteers will do the rest,' Kwan says. 'Let's finish it.'

The cuffs are going on. Get a grip of the breathing first. Steady, two, three, four . . .

Jug Ears has his arms pinned, while Tony, keeping his eyes away from Danny's searching gaze, sees to the restraints. Kwan stands close by, watching intently.

Danny contracts his muscles hard and, when the cuffs swing shut and click, he knows he's probably got slack in at least one of them. Is it enough though?

He makes it look as though they're tight fast. Keep the illusion up, Dad would say. Make it look like they've got you trussed like the proverbial chicken.

Tony's putting a long chain round him now and Danny plants his legs very slightly apart, expanding his quads and hamstrings. Again, you couldn't tell if you weren't looking for it. And now take a deep breath, opening the torso, as big as possible. Probably best to lay it on a bit thick as well. They'd expect that.

'Please . . . I don't know anything. Just let me go. Please.' Struggle a bit.

Pony Tail is looking agitated. He runs a hand over his battered face and grimaces. He turns to say something in Cantonese to Kwan, but Kwan just shakes his head. A few of the other Triads are shuffling uneasily, some looking away.

Danny forces his eyes to gaze out to sea. Keep Tony distracted from what I'm doing with my hands.

Hammerhead clouds are building on the horizon, dark and mean, and he stares towards them, bringing his concentration deeper, his breathing firmer. But it feels like – at any moment – he might lose that control and go to bits and then . . . ? It always happens, Dad used to say. So you just take another breath and let the thought melt. *Thoughts have no substance, Danny. They come, they go, just like that.*

So full focus now. The chain winds around and around. Padlocks clap shut after every other pass. Three of them. Danny eyes them carefully. Two are integrated-type locks. Easy-ish. The third is heavier duty, modular. It'll have a locking dog. Harder. Much harder. But just about do-able given twenty minutes or so. How long will I have? A minute or two at most . . .

The guards open the freezer door. The shelves have been removed to make a space just big enough for him. Danny puts up a token struggle as they force him inside, but he knows full well that the only hope lies ahead. Save energy for that. Follow the trick to its conclusion. At the last minute Jug Ears runs his hands over the cuffs and locks, checking the chains. Tony leans in, looks straight at Danny and shoves him against the back wall of the freezer. But as he does so, he slips something into Danny's trouser pocket. It's heavy, slim. He gives Danny the tiniest of nods.

'Good luck, boy.'

Then the door is slammed shut with a thump. Danny can see the holes in the floor. In the walls. Tiny pinpricks of light shine on him. It's hard to stand straight and the chains feel very heavy. Distinctly he can feel the weight of whatever Tony sleight-of-handed into his jeans pocket. Odd, that.

The screech of gaffer tape being wound round and round the freezer interrupts his thoughts.

Sealing me in. Just take it one lock at a time, he repeats to himself. One lock at a time. He closes his eyes.

Zamora half sits, half slumps against the wall, covered by two machine guns, tears slipping from his eyes. He tries to speak but the words are knotted in his throat.

Laura bites at the tape over her mouth, gagging, eyes wide open in horror as another chain is put under the freezer and brought to a loop on top.

* * *

The camouflage net is dragged away from the deck.

Overhead a crane splutters into life, coughing black smoke into the evening sky. Its arm swings out over the yellow circle of the helipad. The loop is attached to it and then, without any further ceremony, it lifts the freezer – the improvised water torture cell – high up over the ship. It jerks out and over the water, dancing on the chain.

'Do it for me, Danny!' Sing Sing shouts.

'Quiet!' Kwan barks. 'There is no escape.'

The freezer, criss-crossed with black tape, hangs for a moment against the evening. Then Kwan drops his hand, and the whole thing plunges to the sea below.

Ploooomphhhh. It hits the surface, sending up a waterspout that mushrooms over the cell and then sighs back . . .

Not a sound from the freezer.

Laura shuts her eyes tight. He's probably out cold already, stunned by the fall, she thinks. Hope he is. Hope he doesn't know what's happening . . .

The freezer bobs uncertainly on the water for a half-minute or so, and then – quite rapidly – starts to sink. As it does so it drifts slowly from the cargo boat, sliding into the gathering waves.

Half submerged, three quarters . . .

Within the minute it is gone from sight, trailing a string of bubbles on the water. And the evening gathers under the lowering sky.

Behind the tape Laura is sobbing. And in Zamora's eyes there is a rage such as Sing Sing has never seen.

'I'll deal with you lot in minute,' Kwan says, and stomps away towards the bridge.

6 HOW TO DO THE WATER TORTURE ESCAPE

As soon as Danny is sure that the door's not going to be opened again, he gets to work.

Before the hoist is even connected, he's flexing his wrists against the handcuffs, squeezing the bones in his hand, jamming the thumb painfully towards his little finger. You have to be careful because if you manage to get some slack, and then knock the cuffs, you can end up worse off than before. The ratchet will bite tighter and cut off your blood supply. Then comes neuropathy and your hands are useless.

Damn. Not going to be as easy as some. His heart is picking up an insistent beat, blood pulsing faster. Keep calm. Keep calm or it all goes wrong. He stops and breathes up through his feet, qigong style, like Blanco showed him on those distant, dewy mornings.

He hears the crane starting and works his left wrist harder against the cuff. Normally the best place to start. Being right-handed, there's marginally less muscle on the other side. And it was the second to be cuffed, so often just that bit looser.

The chains binding his arms to his sides feel very tight though.

No. The other problems can wait their turn. No reality but the thing you're doing now. Suddenly he loses his balance and slips against the side of the freezer. Feels the whole thing lift and start to sway.

If I can just get this one hand loose, before the drop.

The cell swings crazily for a moment and then steadies itself. One more go at the left wrist. And his hand is free!

First problem solved.

Trying not to think how high he is over the water, he takes up a brace position, crouching down as best he can on the freezer floor, bending his knees for shock absorption. There's a wind getting up, and it sets the cell swaying crazily for a second, makes an eerie whistling as it plays through the holes drilled in the sides. Come on, for God's sake, get it over with . . .

And then he's falling, stomach lurching . . .

It seems to last ridiculously long, that downward rush, but then – more like an explosion than a splash – the cell hits the water, jarring his legs, compressing his back, forcing the wind out of him. It sounds like he's gone straight under, the frothing of the seawater all around. Then they're bobbing back up to the surface . . .

The freezer stands tall for a second, then falls on one side and floats there. Water spouts through the holes. He can feel it soaking his clothes. Taste the salt. Are we sinking yet?

With his left wrist free there's enough slack in the chains to bring that arm around to the front. But try as he might he can't get his hand up to reach for the lockpick. Should have palmed it. Damn.

Water is flooding the cell now. It's a quarter full very quickly. He works the chains like he had watched Dad do countless times. Expand, contract, expand, contract, wriggle.

Now there's a little slack to work with. His back is soaking wet and his legs are under water. Definitely sinking.

Don't think about it.

Half full. It'll be time to take a deep breath very, very soon.

It'll never be possible to get the hand high enough to lift the lockpick over his head. Plan B then. Lift the T-shirt up. It rips a bit. Now get the pick to that first padlock. Need the right hand too. Running out of air. Damn.

The water is up to his neck. He takes a deep breath, blows that right out and then inhales again, as deeply as he possibly can. Time for brute strength – with every fibre of effort he wrenches his right arm around to the front, working it under the chains. It hurts like anything. Forget it.

The water closes over him, foaming in his ears. It's dark now and the freezer is rolling as it slowly descends.

But the lockpick is in his right hand. He fiddles out the saw rake by touch and then he's working it into the plug. No time to feel it carefully. Just rake the thing as hard as possible and try and bounce the pins to the shearline. Keep tension on the lock and work it quickly back and forward. Blot everything else out.

He feels something give. Yes! The first lock's open. That releases the top chains a bit more now. Going to have to get every one of them off otherwise I'll never make the surface. They'll pull me down . . .

It takes vital seconds to locate the second lock in the gloom, but then it goes quickly with the same jagging rake of the pick. He lets the air seep very slowly from his mouth. Almost one bubble at a time. The pressure's building and he's already desperate to take a clean lungful of air.

Got about a minute left.

Wish it wasn't so dark.

Hard to reach the modular lock. He contorts his body, trying to get both hands to it. There it is . . .

Work it with the rake tool again. Harder . . . Won't go. Won't go.

Not thinking straight.

Need to breathe. Lungs . . .

Ears hurt.

Calm. Be calm.

Wait a minute – last lock doesn't do anything. They missed the chain with the shackle! So work the chains, keep working . . .

They're off. Nothing left.

Door now. No idea how to do it.

Maybe thirty seconds.

He kicks frantically at the door, lungs burning, but the gaffer tape seals it rigidly tight. Just then his hand brushes against the object in his pocket. The one Tony slipped him with that slight nod of the head. Feeling in his soaked jeans he finds the thing. Its cold metal fits snugly into the palm of his hand. It must be! The folding pocketknife that Pony Tail used to free their hands on the fishing boat.

He flicks it open by touch, gropes for the corner of the freezer and then jabs the blade into the seal between door and side.

It's through . . . is it?

Tired now . . .

Need to breathe . . . Running out . . . Lungs on fire . . .

He can see stars dancing. Oxygen debt? But the blade is doing its work. He runs it down the length of the door. Then, strength ebbing away, back up again. Hard work. Very hard . . .

Think I'm blacking out . . . And so close . . .

As if from a great distance he sees himself struggling, now upside down, spotlit, hair waving like seaweed. So tired . . . The skull and butterflies are dancing in the black water. Transient.

And the door's just about . . .

. . . Can't.

7 HOW TO SWEAR PROFUSELY

Sing Sing comes along the side of the deck, her head bowed, feeling as desperate as she has ever felt in her fourteen years. She coughs out every Cantonese swear word she can ever remember hearing as she grew up on the margins of the world of the Triads. Then she empties off her English vocabulary too. Unspeakable acts, unpleasant things. Even Zamora raises his eyes in shock.

The gang members are silent, ill at ease, as they escort her, Zamora and Aunt Laura back towards the crew quarters.

She lifts her head for a moment. Looks out at the water. The night is pooling across it and clouds roll in to block out the sky.

She comes to an abrupt stop. There's a lifebelt on the rail here – and she grabs it and, more as a gesture than anything else, hurls it as far as she can out over the side.

The man behind shakes his head and jabs her with his machine pistol in the back. Behind them Pony Tail watches the lifebelt as it floats away into the gloom. Thoughtful . . .

They sit dejectedly in the bulkhead storeroom.

When Zamora peels the tape from Laura's mouth she has nothing to say. Just puts her head in her hands and sets her shoulders heaving silently.

'Maybe there's still hope,' Zamora says.

'Come off it, Major . . .' she sobs.

'I managed to get a message to Ricard,' Sing Sing says. 'At least, I hope I have. I had to bribe one of the Triads on Cheung Chau to call Ricard . . . but, I guess too late. Sorry, sorry, sorry.' She kicks at the ground.

'That makes three of us,' Zamora says.

8 HOW TO COME TO THE SURFACE

. . . As if he's watching himself in super-slow motion.

As if – because time is up – he suddenly has all the time in the world. Serenity embracing him in the blue-black depths.

Which way's up? Doesn't really matter. Let go . . .

A school of red fish ghost across his eyes. Very close.

The cell falls away, a pale shadow fading to nothing. That must be down then. Or is it up?

The last of the air escaping.

Another choking mouthful of water. Swallowing . . .

This is drowning then. Dammit.

And then it comes to him in one crystalline, pure memory.

That day when Dad failed to escape from the water torture cell, there was something wrong. They'd painted the equipment the evening before and left it sitting in the wings near the processional door. That bright-red paint looked so nice . . .

. . . And the next day it was bone dry.

But when one of the Klowns came rushing to help Dad, leering in his skull mask, there was a red smear on his trouser knee. Not big. But exactly the same red.

The Klowns hadn't helped paint the thing. So this one must have been near it that night . . .

It must have been sabotage.

A pulse of energy from somewhere. I'll get out of this – I'll surface. Find the trail. Find out what happened.

It feels like his lungs are pressed flat, useless, as he tumbles in the sea's grip – but now he steadies himself and then kicks towards what he hopes is up.

Towards life.

Not just because he wants to live, but because now he knows he has a hope of finding the truth.

Another mouthful of black water forces its way to his stomach. He pulls loose the ragged tour T-shirt and leaves it to the depths. The fateful tour itinerary on its back – pale butterflies and empty-eyed skull – disappearing into emptiness.

Another kick from his exhausted legs . . . pushing up, up.

Where is it? Where's the surface? How long has he been under . . . ? Come on. Come on!

. . . And Danny breaks the skin of the waves, spluttering, choking, shaking, drowning, not drowning. Treading water.

The heavy bulk of the carrier stands some hundred metres away, the island silhouetted beyond that. There's a dim glow of light from the boat but otherwise not much else. Maybe – maybe – far off to the north-east, a light on the water. But it could be a low star where the air's still clear. It's swamped by the waves running before the oncoming storm.

Mustn't go under now. So tired though.

Then something nudges the back of his head and he freezes, imagining sharks or a boat from the ship. It nudges him again and he reaches around – and has his arm through the orange and white lifebelt.

The sea is getting choppier.

Bring it on, thinks Danny. Bring it on.

He floats there for a while. Coughs up some water

and lets his head clear.

And then a broad smile cracks across his face – and he feels like yelling at the top of his voice: I did it! I did the water torture escape! Me. Danny Woo . . .

He slaps at a wave joyously, and shakes his head.

And then starts to kick determinedly towards the ship as the first of the rain peppers the water.

9 HOW TO EXHIBIT DECENCY

No one sees or hears him coming.

The decks have cleared as the rain squalls hit the boat. Two guards duck for shelter under the lee of a lifeboat – and so don't see Danny reaching the anchor chain.

They don't see him climb it, as easy as you like despite the weather. After all, it's only like going up a rope at the Mysterium, and he could do that before he could walk.

Struggling to light their cigarettes, the guards don't see him make the deck of the ship and glide into the rain-lashed shadows.

The plan of the crew quarters is clear in his head. Tony's pocketknife is open in his right hand, blade jagged and broken in his desperate escape from the freezer. Eyes blazing, senses alert.

No one's looking for him. So no one sees him . . .

He crosses beneath the boom of the crane, ducks under an awning as a Triad sprints towards shelter, flip-flops splashing on the deck.

Through the door and into the first corridor. There's not a soul in sight, but a tangle of voices not far off. He lets the door close noiselessly, then drops down the companionway in one smooth jump, hands gliding on the rails.

Left here, past the galley. A cacophony inside. Dinner time presumably.

Think of nothing and nobody can see you, Dad used to say, so that's what he does. He shoves every thought away and becomes nothing but silent movement . . .

Another stairway, sinking into the heart of the ship, and then down the corridor to the room which is acting as a brig. No lock – just the ring handle on the outside of the watertight door.

He grips the rough metal and heaves.

It's surprisingly stiff and almost takes the last drop of his strength.

Laura is the first to look up and see him. Her face is a picture, jaw dropping slack – and then she reaches to shake Zamora by the shoulder. Sing Sing leaps to her feet in one acrobatic flip, hands flying to her face to suppress a scream of relief. The rain and wind dashing at the ship, affording them some cover, but they all have the sense to keep their voices down . . .

Soaked, bare-chested, Danny slips into the brig and closes the door behind him. His arms and chest are lacerated, the cuffs still dangling from his right wrist and he looks close to exhaustion. But still he smiles – the sense of triumph still pumping in his body.

The Major staggers to his feet: 'I knew it! *Caramba*, I knew you could do it.'

Laura shakes her head and hugs Danny just as hard as the day of the explosion.

'Blast Houdini,' she says. 'You're the greatest. Of all time!'

And Zamora beams, wiping a tear from his eye. 'You've joined the greats, Danny. If your dad could see you now!'

'We've still got to get out of here,' Danny says. 'All of us together. In one piece.'

'We need more help,' Laura says, checking the corridor. 'I think I know where we can find it. Laundry. This way.'

* * *

The corridor stretches ahead, voices echoing over the weather outside.

'Let's take it steady—' Laura starts to say.

'Forget that!' Zamora says. 'I'm an angry dwarf right now.'

He steams ahead and, wheeling round a corner, goes full speed into one of the pirates. The man has dinner on his mind – not enraged dwarf strongmen – and before he has time to register what's happening, Zamora has lowered his head, increased his gallop and butted the gangster full force in the chest. The air rushes from his lungs in a whoosh and he sinks to the ground, mouth gasping for air.

'*Buenos noches*,' Zamora says and, taking the man's cleaver, thumps him on the back of the head with the handle.

'See? I'm showing restraint here! Decency!'

He rushes on down the corridor, closely followed by the others.

Three guards are sitting round a folding table outside the laundry room in a fug of smoke. Their eyes are fixed on the cards in their hands, and the money piled on the table in front of them. So they don't see Zamora's whirlwind attack.

He has the first two grabbed by the scruff of their necks before they can struggle from their seats.

'Nobody messes with Mister Danny,' Zamora growls, and brings their heads smartly together. An ear-splitting crack resounds between the tight walls and they're slumping across the money and cards and beer cans, out for the count.

The third Dragon is lifting his gun, aiming at Zamora's neck. But then a sharp burst of Cantonese stops the man in his tracks.

It's Pony Tail. And he has his pistol jammed against the back of his fellow Dragon's head, whose eyes bulge in surprise.

'*Maih yuka!*' he says, '*Don't move!*'

'I don't think your pal is bluffing,' Zamora says. 'I'd do what he says.'

The man lets his gun fall with a clatter to the floor and raises his hands slowly.

Pony Tail turns to look at Danny. There's a smile at the corners of his mouth.

'You are number-one amazing kid,' he says.

'I should punch the stuffing out of you,' Zamora says. 'Again.'

'No,' Danny says. 'I couldn't have done it without him.'

He hands the folded knife back to Pony Tail. 'I'm sorry. The blade snapped as I was cutting myself free.'

Laura puts a hand on Tony's shoulder. 'We'll give you the benefit. Open this door for us and Major Zamora will let bygones be bygones.'

There are ten or so crew members inside, a mix of Chinese and Philippinos. They look weary, hungry, their cheeks hollowed.

A heavily built man steps forward from amongst them, face set resolutely. His face is black and blue, one eye closing tight from a nasty blow. Blood dried on his white shirt. He eyes Pony Tail with contempt but reads the situation quickly, before turning to Zamora.

'I am Captain Zhang. Who the hell are you?'

'We're cleaning up the ship,' Zamora says. 'Care to help?'

'The bridge,' the captain says. 'We'll try and take control. Seal ourselves in and get radio help.'

His men gather what weapons are available: a meat cleaver, two guns.

Danny looks round to ask Pony Tail to help them, but the man has slipped away into the shadows. Just the quick flight of footsteps echoing in the distance . . .

'That rat's going to raise the alarm,' Sing Sing says.

Danny listens to the fading sound. 'No, I don't think so. He's making a break for it . . .'

10 HOW TO STORM THE BRIDGE

Captain Zhang leads them through the bowels of the ship, past cabins, storerooms, down long service gangways that still hold the heat of the engine, the humidity of the muggy day just gone.

No one talks.

Danny is lagging towards the back, still soaked from the immersion, still short of breath from the near drowning. His right arm doesn't feel good after wrenching it against the chains, and his vision keeps flickering white as exhaustion tugs away at his mind.

But I'll be OK, he thinks. And feels it suddenly with certainty. Whatever happens, I'll be OK. We'll be OK.

They have come to the bottom of a steep ladder.

'Bridge directly up here,' Captain Zhang whispers. 'Tactics?'

'No tactics,' Zamora says. 'We attack!'

And he's away, up the rungs, closely followed by

Zhang and his men, with Laura and Sing Sing struggling to catch up.

Danny suddenly feels as though his legs won't go any further. The tiredness and shock and cold have got him now. He slumps down on the bottom step, trying to control the shakes that are creeping up his legs.

From above there's an eruption of sound. A burst of clattering gunfire, jarringly loud. Everyone shouting at once and the thump and crack of close quarters fighting. Stench of cordite in the air.

Zamora shouts above everyone, 'That's for Mister Danny! And that's another one!'

A man comes tumbling down the companionway and Danny just has the wits left to dodge the body as it crumples unconscious at his feet.

More gunfire stuttering. Single shots. Breaking glass.

A distant splash from outside – and then the alarm is sounding and Danny can hear footsteps approaching fast.

He gathers his strength, trying to summon some life back into his legs and starts to climb heavily to the battle raging above . . .

* * *

It's a quick intense fight. Kwan and the Black Dragon are caught off guard. Zamora lets loose, fists flailing, tattoos jumping, sending one – then two – Triads sagging to the ground. A third hurtles through the bridge window into the sea far below.

And Zhang's men want revenge too. 'They soon have two more Triads down and have sent the others scuttling from the bridge. Amongst the confusion of gunshot and close-hand fighting Laura makes straight for Kwan. He pulls a gun from his belt but Sing Sing is there, kicking it violently from his hand, and then she and Laura have him held tight against the ship's control panel. Sing Sing pushes her face right into Kwan's.

'You are just about the worst taxi driver I have ever come across,' she hisses. 'I'm going to think of something really unpleasant to do to you. Really unpleasant. And then I'm going to turn you over to Charlie.'

'Charlie's dead,' Kwan whispers. 'I saw to it myself—'

But then he sees Danny stumbling up onto the bridge, and his eyes almost pop from their sockets. As if a ghost has materialized from out of thin air. Kwan's mouth works frantically but can make no sound.

'Seal the bridge,' Zhang shouts. 'All lights up.'

'What do you mean about Charlie?' Sing Sing shouts.

But she's interrupted by raking gunfire from outside. The bridge window detonates in a shower of glass sending them all crouching to the ground. Kwan takes his moment, wrenches himself free and makes a dash for the door to the deck beyond. There's a searing whoosh in the cabin – a blinding blue line of fire that arcs across the bridge and strikes Kwan on the upper back as he makes his escape. He screams as the flare hits and then he's spun around by the force and propelled over the rail to the sea below. The blue light burns itself out on the deck, casting an eerie light over everything.

'Get the radio up,' Zhang shouts, the flaregun still gripped tight in his hand. 'Put out a Mayday.'

But now, in the sudden lull, they hear the thrumming of an engine approaching at speed, the smack of bow on wave.

Strong searchlights rake the camouflage netting. It's as bright as broad daylight on the bridge and a megaphone barks through the night, an authoritative Chinese voice.

And then a different voice in English, with a slight accent. 'You are all under arrest. Stay where you are.

Drop your weapons. This is the Hong Kong Police. And Interpol. Inspector Ricard. The Chinese Navy and OCTB have you surrounded.'

'We've done it, Danny,' Laura shouts.

She looks round. Danny has slumped to the floor, eyes clamped shut, and the Major is crouched over him, slapping his cheek.

'Mister Danny? Mister Danny?'

The rain squall beats against the ship.

'Danny?'

There's more shouting outside on the deck. One long, low dragon-like roar of thunder and then silence returns again.

'He's still breathing,' Zamora says. 'Come on, Mister Danny. Get a blanket, someone, he's shivering like anything.'

Danny half smiles. And opens his eyes.

Electric green, deepest brown, they flash in the glow of the searchlights. He blinks hard, trying to work out where he is. Trying to make sense of the world.

'Did I get out in time?'

'You did it, Mister Danny. You did the escape. The Chinese water torture! Just wait till I tell the old Mysterium crowd about this. Blanco and Rosa are going to freak out!'

Danny looks around at the wreckage of the bridge.

Yes, it all makes sense, he thinks. At least *some* of it does now.

11 HOW TO SEE THE WONDER

The rain has cleared to leave a cool, calm morning. The pre-dawn breaking green on the horizon as the police launch surges towards the harbour.

Danny is standing in the wheelhouse, wrapped in an aluminium blanket, next to Ricard. Despite the sea crossing, the night, the arrest of most of the Black Dragon, the Interpol man looks immaculate as ever in his white suit. Just a hint of tiredness in the lines around his eyes.

Laura and Sing Sing are on the front deck, watching the buildings heave themselves skywards in the first light, the whaleback hills rising up from the sea.

And in the cabin below Zamora is sitting with the police, watching over Jug Ears and some of the other half-drowned and bloodied Triads, fighting sleep, rousing himself every now and then to list a few more of their shortcomings. It's a very long and specific list . . . and he's only halfway through.

* * *

Danny turns to Ricard. 'What about Kwan?'

'No sign. We'll keep a boat searching, but he's probably shark meat now.'

'Did you know about him?'

'Heavens, no. He was completely off our radar, as far as I can tell.'

'And Lo?'

'He's suspended and under arrest by Internal Affairs. Should go down for a long time. We've just been trying to get enough on him. You'll be our star witness. And Laura.'

'Monsieur Ricard, what do you really know about the Forty Nine? Tell me.'

'I'm still not sure one way or another, Danny. Maybe Kwan was all hot air and bluster – or maybe there *is* something to this fairy tale after all. Maybe it has *become* real and Kwan was just one of those dots on the diagram. In that case he'll be replaced now with someone else . . .'

His voice trails off.

'There's something you're holding back,' Danny says.

'Well, I need to warn you. If the Forty Nine *are* real – and your dad thought as much – then sitting at the heart of it all is someone they call Centre. But we have no idea who or where that person is. He – or she – might be the one who ordered Kwan to put you in that freezer. It's not impossible that Laura was lured to pursue this story . . . I will need to make urgent inquiries – see if the trail leads to a real threat. Or an imagined one.' He looks away towards the gathering light. 'But if Centre exists, we must suspect he was linked to the death of your parents. The improvised water torture and all that . . .'

At last!

'So *you* don't think the fire was an accident either.'

'I have my doubts. Just never had any evidence to pursue things.'

'I knew it. I knew the police missed something.'

'But what, I wonder?' Ricard looks at him searchingly. 'There's something you aren't telling *me* now, *mon brave*.'

'Oh, it's nothing.' Danny shakes his head. 'Nothing at all really.'

But he's thinking about Dad's *Escape Book*. He wants to get home and look at it again. See what is buried there in the code. And he's thinking about that Khaos Klown and the smear of paint . . . My secret, he thinks. At least for now. For once I have some control over who knows what. Some power. And I want to keep it to myself.

'Can you tell me more about my dad and you? The work he did for you?'

'Not really, Danny.'

'I need to know.'

'I'm sorry, but I can't. But I can tell you that he was a good man. Very brave.'

Danny nods. He wants to ask more but can see Ricard will go no further. 'Can I at least contact you if I need to?'

'Of course. Any time. Come on, forget about it for a little while. You need to recover. Look, the sun's just about coming up.'

Laura comes in from the deck. Her usual composure regained.

'Sing Sing's taking Chow's death awfully well. Says she'll be OK.'

Danny nods, looking out to the deck where Sing Sing still stands, her hair flying in the wind. As if feeling his gaze, she turns and looks back at him. Smiling determinedly through her own emotion. Someone who feels like him. Someone who might just understand what he has been through. That alone makes the last few days' nightmarish effort worthwhile. He smiles back.

'I'll go and see if she's OK.'

'You do that, Danny boy.'

Danny glances at his watch. The date shows thirty-one.

The thirty-first of October.

'Hey, it's Halloween. You know what that means?'

'Trick or treat?'

'It's the anniversary of Houdini's death. We used to do something to mark that . . . in the old days. Dad would do something in his honour. Always.'

'Then let's do that,' Laura says. 'How about dinner – Hong Kong style?'

'I'll see what Sing Sing wants to do. Whatever she wants is fine with me.'

He goes out onto the deck and glances back at their wake. Somewhere far behind, just over the horizon, is the place where he pulled off his desperate bid for freedom, watching the freezer falling into the limitless depths. Seems so hard to believe . . .

And it makes him think of Dad and the way his own meticulously planned version of the water torture went wrong. Much later that night – after the failed escape – Danny had sat up with him, refusing to go to bed.

At first he had felt confusion. How could Dad fail? In front of all those people? Wasn't he the greatest living exponent of the art? If he could fail – then anyone could. So there were no guarantees in the world . . .

And they talked about that – and the fact that you have to let your mistakes teach you so that they're not wasted. *You only learn to walk the wire by falling.* And that led to other things and they went on long into the night, discussing routines and tricks. Great escapes and their risks and difficulties and how even people like Houdini or great walkers like Wallenda eventually slipped up and succumbed to the inevitable. Eventually Danny said, 'Why do you do it, Dad?'

'What, old son?'

'The danger. Injuries. Dislocating things. The hard work.'

'I would hope that's obvious,' Dad said. 'But I'll spell it out for you. You've heard of Einstein, right?'

'Yep.'

'A genius in anyone's book. Well, he said something like this: "The most beautiful thing we can experience is the *mysterious*. The person who can no longer stand rapt in wonder and awe is as good as dead. Their eyes are closed".'

He sighed. '*That's* why I do it, that's why *we* do it. We help to keep the mystery.'

And then he smiled broadly.

'Got to keep the mystery, Danny. Because that keeps us alive.'

Danny looks up from the memory. The sun is cracking through the clouds and Hong Kong shimmers into life before them in all its towering glory.

It's like the most amazing conjuring trick. The world reborn again.

He watches it unfold, his eyes alive with the wonder.

GLOSSARY

Archaos
French circus group who tore up the rule book. Founded in 1986 by Pierrot Bidon, Archaos threw chainsaws, punk, flame and fake blood into the traditional circus mix – reinvigorating and reimagining life under the big top.

Cantonese
Chinese dialect – mainly spoken in Hong Kong, Guangzhou and overseas Chinese communities across the world. Shares written characters with Mandarin but sounds very different.

catcher
On the flying trapeze, the person responsible for catching the flyer.

cavaletti
Guy wires used to stabilize tight and high wires.

charivari	Meaning 'various jokes' the term for a short, lively clown act often performed between other acts.
Cirque du Soleil	French Canadian circus company founded in 1984 blending street performance with art and traditional skills. Now plays to tens of thousands of people worldwide every year.
Cyr wheel	Large metal hoop in which an acrobat balances and then spins and turns somersaults.
David Blaine	American illusionist and magician famed for his feats of endurance and psychological strength. Blaine has been encased in a block of ice for 63 hours, buried alive, and lived without food in a glass box for 44 days.
death walk	Walking a steeply inclined tight wire.
escapology	The art of escaping from any kind of restraint – often in dangerous and time limited circumstances. Performers like Houdini escaped from handcuffs, straightjackets, mailbags, locked prison cells, chains, coffins, burning buildings . . .
flyer	On the flying trapeze the artist who lets go of the bar and flies . . .
force	In magic, the art of making an audience member make a choice that seems

random, but is actually controlled by the performer.

hellstromism   The reading by light touch of slight involuntary muscle movements in a subject, caused by that subject thinking about a direction or movement.

hemisphere   The aerial space immediately under the big top where aerial acts are performed.

high wire   Wirewalking act performed at considerable height and therefore risk. Often in public spaces, sometimes illegally.

hypnosis   A vast and controversial field ranging from stage hypnosis, where susceptible audience members seemingly act under trance, to hypnotherapy, used to help phobias and trauma. Some claim the effects of hypnosis are genuine mental states, others that a combination of suggestibility and willingness to please are at work.

human cannonball Springloaded cannon that propels the performer across the arena. First performed in 1877 by a 14-year-old girl called Zazel. Numerous fatalities have subsequently occurred to human cannonballs.

josser   Term from British circus and travelling communities meaning non circus person.

Karl Wallenda	Member of the most famous high wire family, the Flying Wallendas, famed for their seven-person pyramid. Karl fell to his death in 1978 in Puerto Rico.
living burial	Famous stunt performed by Houdini that nearly cost him his life in its first and most basic version, clawing his way out of an earth filled grave.
Mandarin	Standard form of Chinese spoken across large parts of mainland China.
New Circus	Modern circus form that balances traditional skills with attention to performance and artistry and avoids animal acts. Sometimes called Contemporary or Alt Circus.
palm	In magic a sleight of hand action that secretly picks up and hides an object.
roustabout	Locally hired staff who pitch, rig and strike a circus.
Shearline	Lockpicking term – when all the pins in a lock align to allow the mechanism to open.
slack wire	A wire or rope rigged at less tension than tight wire allowing performers to bounce and do acrobatics.
Triad	Secret criminal societies still active in many parts of the world with Chinese communities. Originally formed from

groups dedicated to protecting China, they concentrated in Hong Kong after the Communist revolution of 1949.

voltige — performers join their hands into a grid support (known as a 'chair'), and throw another acrobat in a series of increasingly high somersaults.

wall of death — Circular, vertically walled motorcycle track. Riders fly around horizontally to the ground – if they keep the right speed and line.

Water Torture Cell — Houdini's greatest stunt. Also known as the Chinese Water Torture. Locked and shackled upside down in a full tank of water, the escapologist wriggles free before running out of air. Genuinely dangerous and not to be attempted at home. Try juggling eggs instead for a 'frisson of catastrophe'.

ACKNOWLEDGEMENTS

The story of Danny and his friends (and enemies) in the Mysterium would not have come to light without the help and support of many people.

In particular, at Hodder Children's Books, I'd like to thank Beverley Birch for her foresight and Jon Appleton for his insight.

I'm also very grateful to my agent, Kirsty McLachlan, for helping to plant the seed of this idea and for nurturing it, and to my brother, Marcus, for his constant encouragement.

It's not always easy living around aspiring and perspiring writers, and for that reason I give heartfelt thanks to my wife Isabel, and my two boys – Joseph and William – for their fortitude, forbearance and love. And for some of the better ideas in these pages.